WILLIAM SEWARD BURROUGHS was born in 1914 in St Louis, Missouri, the son of the inventor of the adding machine. After graduating in English literature from Harvard in 1936, he drifted from one pursuit to another, attending medical school in Vienna and graduate school in anthropology at Harvard, and worked variously as an adman, bartender, and exterminator in Chicago and New York City.

His most famous novel, *The Naked Lunch*, first appeared in the plain green covers of *The Traveller's Companion Series* of Girodias' Olympia Press in Paris in 1959. At that time he was virtually unknown. Real fame – or notoriety – did not come until the 1962 Edinburgh Festival, when Mary McCarthy innocently named Burroughs among the three or four contemporary writers whose work interested her. The reaction this provoked among the press soon established him as an international *cause célèbre: The Naked Lunch* became as much a part of the American avante garde of the sixties as Cage's 4′ 33″ and Rauschenberg's stuffed Angora goat.

A member of the American Academy and Institute of Arts and Letters and a Commander of the Order of Arts and Letters in France, Burroughs now divides his time between New York City and Lawrence, Kansas. His novels include *Nova Express*, *The Soft Machine*, *The Place of Dead Roads*, *Dead Fingers Talk* and *Cities of the Red Night*. This last book and *A William Burroughs Reader* are published in Picador.

Also by William S. Burroughs
in Picador

Cities of the Red Night
A William Burroughs Reader edited by John Calder

William S. Burroughs

QUEER

PICADOR
published by **Pan Books**

First published in 1985 by Viking Penguin Inc.
First Picador edition published in Great Britain by Pan Books Ltd
This paperback edition published 1986 by Pan Books Ltd,
Cavaye Place, London SW10 9PG
9 8 7 6 5 4 3 2
© William S. Burroughs 1985
ISBN 0 330 30016 4
Photoset by Parker Typesetting Service, Leicester
Printed and bound in Great Britain by
Cox & Wyman Ltd, Reading

Introduction

When I lived in Mexico City at the end of the 1940s, it was a city of one million people, with clear sparkling air and the sky that special shade of blue that goes so well with circling vultures, blood and sand – the raw menacing pitiless Mexican blue. I liked Mexico City from the day of my first visit there. In 1949, it was a cheap place to live, with a large foreign colony, fabulous whorehouses and restaurants, cockfights and bullfights, and every conceivable diversion. A single man could live well there for two dollars a day. My New Orleans case for heroin and marijuana possession looked so unpromising that I decided not to show up for the court date, and I rented an apartment in a quiet, middle-class neighborhood of Mexico City.

I knew that under the statute of limitations I could not return to the United States for five years, so I applied for Mexican citizenship and enrolled in some courses in Mayan and Mexican archaeology at Mexico City College. The G.I. Bill paid for my books and tuition, and a seventy-five-dollar-per-month living allowance. I thought I might go into farming, or perhaps open a bar on the American border.

The City appealed to me. The slum areas compared

favorably with anything in Asia for sheer filth and poverty. People would shit all over the street, then lie down and sleep in it with the flies crawling in and out of their mouths. Entrepreneurs, not infrequently lepers, built fires on street corners and cooked up hideous, stinking, nameless messes of food, which they dispensed to passersby. Drunks slept right on the sidewalks of the main drag, and no cops bothered them. It seemed to me that everyone in Mexico had mastered the art of minding his own business. If a man wanted to wear a monocle or carry a cane, he did not hesitate to do it, and no one gave him a second glance. Boys and young men walked down the street arm in arm and no one paid them any mind. It wasn't that people didn't care what others thought; it simply would not occur to a Mexican to expect criticism from a stranger, nor to criticize the behaviour of others.

Mexico was basically an Oriental culture that reflected two thousand years of disease and poverty and degradation and stupidity and slavery and brutality and psychic and physical terrorism. It was sinister and gloomy and chaotic, with the special chaos of a dream. No Mexican really knew any other Mexican, and when a Mexican killed someone (which happened often), it was usually his best friend. Anyone who felt like it carried a gun, and I read of several occasions where drunken cops, shooting at the habitués of a bar, were themselves shot by armed civilians. As authority figures, Mexican cops ranked with streetcar conductors.

All officials were corruptible, income tax was very low, and medical treatment was extremely reasonable, because the doctors advertised and cut their prices. You could get a clap cured for $2.40, or buy the penicillin and shoot it yourself. There were no regulations curtailing self-medication, and needles and syringes could be bought anywhere. This was in the time of Alemán, when the *mordida* was king, and a pyramid of bribes reached from the cop on the beat up to the Presidente. Mexico City was also the murder capital of the world, with the highest per-capita homicide rate. I remember newspaper stories every day, like these:

A *campesino* is in from the country, waiting for a bus: linen pants, sandals made from a tire, a wide sombrero, a machete at his belt. Another man is also waiting, dressed in a suit, looking at his wrist watch, muttering angrily. The *campesino* whips out his machete and cuts the man's head clean off. He later told police: 'He was giving me looks *muy feo* and finally I could not contain myself.' Obviously the man was annoyed because the bus was late, and was looking down the road for the bus, when the *campesino* misinterpreted his action, and the next thing a head rolls in the gutter, grimacing horribly and showing gold teeth.

Two *campesinos* are sitting disconsolate by the roadside. They have no money for breakfast. But look: a boy leading several goats. One *campesino* picks up a rock and bashes the boy's brains out. They take the goats to the nearest village and sell them. They are eating breakfast when they are apprehended by the police.

A man lives in a little house. A stranger asks him how to find the road for Ayahuasca. 'Ah, this way, *señor*.' He is leading the man around and around: 'The road is right here.' Suddenly he realizes he hasn't any idea where the road is, and why should he be bothered? So he picks up a rock and kills his tormentor.

Campesinos took their toll with rock and machete. More murderous were the politicians and off-duty cops, each with his .45 automatic. One learned to hit the deck. Here is another actual story: A gun-toting *político* hears his girl is cheating, meeting someone in this cocktail lounge.

Some American kid just happens in and sits next to her, when the macho bursts in: '*¡CHINGOA!*' Hauls out his .45 and blasts the kid right off his bar stool. They drag the body outside and down the street a ways. When the cops arrive, the bartender shrugs and mops his bloody bar, and say only: '*Malos, esos muchachos!*' ('Those bad boys!')

Every country has its own special Shits, like the Southern law-man counting his Nigger notches, and the sneering Mexican macho is certainly up there when it comes to sheer ugliness. And many of the Mexican middle class are about as awful as any bourgeoisie in the world. I remember that in Mexico the narcotic scripts were bright yellow, like a thousand-dollar bill, or a dishonorable discharge from the Army. One time Old Dave and I tried to fill such a script, which he had obtained quite legitimately from the Mexican government. The first pharmacist we hit jerked back snarling from such a sight: '*¡No prestamos servicio a los viciosos!*' ('We do not serve dope fiends!')

From one *farmacía* to another we walked, getting sicker with ever step: 'No, *señor*. . .' We must have walked for miles.

'Never been in this neighborhood before.'

'Well, let's try one more.'

Finally we entered a tiny hole-in-the-wall *farmacía*. I pulled out the *receta*, and a gray-haired lady smiled at me. The pharmacist looked at the script, and said, 'Two minutes, *señor*.'

We sat down to wait. There were geraniums in the window. A small boy brought me a glass of water, and a cat rubbed against my leg. After awhile the pharmacist returned with our morphine.

'*Gracias, señor*.'

Outside, the neighborhood now seemed enchanted:

Little *farmacías* in a market, crates and stalls outside, a *pulquería* on the corner. Kiosks selling fried grasshoppers and peppermint candy black with flies. Boys in from the country in spotless white linen and rope sandals, with faces of burnished copper and fierce innocent black eyes, like exotic animals, of a dazzling sexless beauty. Here is a boy with sharp features and black skin, smelling of vanilla, a gardenia behind his ear. Yes, you found a Johnson, but you waded through Shitville to find him. You always do. Just when you think the earth is exclusively populated by Shits, you meet a Johnson.

One day there was a knock on my door at eight in the morning. I went to the door in my pyjamas, and there was an inspector from Immigration.

'Get your clothes on. You're under arrest.'

It seemed the woman next door had turned in a long report on my drunk and disorderly behavior, and also there was something wrong with my papers and where was the Mexican wife I was supposed to have? The Immigration officers were all set to throw me in jail to await deportation as an undesirable alien. Of course, everything could be straightened out with some money, but my interviewer was the head of the deporting department and he wouldn't go for peanuts. I finally had to get up off of two hundred dollars. As I walked home from the Immigration Office, I imagined what I might have had to pay if I had really had an investment in Mexico City.

I thought of the constant problems the three American owners of the Ship Ahoy encountered. The cops came in all the time for a *mordida*, and then came the sanitary inspectors, then more cops trying to get some-

thing on the joint so they could take a real bite. They took
the waiter downtown and beat the shit out of him. They
wanted to know where was Kelly's body stashed? How
many women been raped in the joint? Who brought in
the weed? And so on. Kelly was an American hipster
who had been shot in the Ship Ahoy six months before,
had recovered, and was now in the U.S. Army. No
woman was ever raped there, and no one ever smoked
weed there. By now I had entirely abandoned my plans
to open a bar in Mexico.

An addict has little regard for his image. He wears the
dirtiest, shabbiest clothes, and feels no need to call
attention to himself. During my period of addiction in
Tangiers, I was known as 'El Hombre Invisible', The
Invisible Man. This disintegration of self-image often
results in an indiscriminate image hunger. Billie Holli-
day said she knew she was off junk when she stopped
watching TV. In my first novel, *Junky*, the protagonist
'Lee' comes across as integrated and self-contained, sure
of himself and where he is going. In *Queer* he is disin-
tegrated, desperately in need of contact, completely
unsure of himself and of his purpose.

The difference of course is simple: Lee on junk is
coveted, protected and also severely limited. Not only
does junk short-circuit the sex drive, it also blunts emotional reactions to the vanishing point, depending on the
dosage. Looking back over the action of *Queer*, that
hallucinated month of acute withdrawal takes on a
hellish glow of menace and evil drifting out of neon-lit
cocktail bars, the ugly violence, the .45 always just under
the surface. On junk I was insulated, didn't drink, didn't
go out much, just shot up and waited for the next shot.

When the cover is removed, everything that has been held in check by junk spills out. The withdrawing addict is subject to the emotional excesses of a child or an adolescent, regardless of his actual age. And the sex drive returns in full force. Men of sixty experience wet dreams and spontaneous orgasms (an extremely unpleasant experience, *agaçant* as the French say, putting the teeth on edge). Unless the reader keeps this in mind, the metamorphosis of Lee's character will appear as inexplicable or psychotic. Also bear in mind that the withdrawal syndrome is self-limiting, lasting no more than a month. And Lee has a phase of excessive drinking, which exacerbates all the worst and most dangerous aspects of the withdrawal sickness: reckless, unseemly, outrageous, maudlin – in a word, appalling – behavior.

After withdrawal, the organism readjusts and stabilizes at a pre-junk level. In the narrative, this stabilization is finally reached during the South American trip. No junk is available, nor any other drug, after the paregoric of Panama. Lee's drinking has dwindled to several good stiff ones at sundown. Not so different from the Lee of the later *Yage Letters*, except for the phantom presence of Allerton.

So I had written *Junky*, and the motivation for that was comparatively simple: to put down in the most accurate and simple terms my experiences as an addict. I was hoping for publication, money, recognition. Kerouac had published *The Town and the City* at the time I started writing *Junky*. I remember writing in a letter to him, when his book was published, that money and fame were now assured. As you can see, I knew nothing about the writing business at the time.

My motivations to write *Queer* were more complex, and are not clear to me at the present time. Why should I wish to chronicle so carefully these extremely painful and unpleasant and lacerating memories? While it was I who wrote *Junky*, I feel that I was being written in *Queer*. I was also taking pains to ensure further writing, so as to set the record straight: writing as inoculation. As soon as something is written, it loses the power of surprise, just as a virus loses its advantage when a weakened virus has created alerted antibodies. So I achieved some immunity from further perilous ventures along these lines by writing my experience down.

At the beginning of the *Queer* manuscript fragment, having returned from the insulation of junk to the land of the living like a frantic inept Lazarus, Lee seems determined to score, in the sexual sense of the word. There is something curiously systematic and unsexual about his quest for a suitable sex object, crossing one prospect after another off a list which seems compiled with ultimate failure in mind. On some very deep level he does not want to succeed, but will go to any length to avoid the realization that he is not really looking for sex contact.

But Allerton was definitely *some* sort of contact. And what was the contact that Lee was looking for? Seen from here, a very confused concept that had nothing to do with Allerton as a character. While the addict is indifferent to the impression he creates in others, during withdrawal he may feel the compulsive need for an audience, and this is clearly what Lee seeks in Allerton: an audience, the acknowledgement of his performance, which of course is a mask, to cover a shocking disintegration. So he invents a frantic attention-getting format which he calls the Routine: shocking, funny, riveting. 'It is an Ancient Mariner, and he stoppeth one of three . . .'

The performance takes the form of routines: fantasies about Chess Players, the Texas Oilman, Corn Hole Gus's Used-Slave Lot. In *Queer*, Lee addresses these routines to an actual audience. Later, as he develops as a writer, the audience becomes internalized. But the same mechanism that produced A.J. and Doctor Benway, the same creative impulse, is dedicated to Allerton, who is forced into the role of approving Muse, in which he feels understandably uncomfortable.

What Lee is looking for is contact or recognition, like a photon emerging from the haze of insubstantiality to leave an indelible recording in Allerton's consciousness. Failing to find an adequate observer, he is threatened by painful dispersal, like an unobserved photon. Lee does not know that he is already committed to writing, since this is the only way he has of making an indelible record, whether Allerton is inclined to observe or not. Lee is being inexorably pressed into the world of fiction. He has already made the choice between his life and his work.

The manuscript trails off in Puyo, End of the Road town . . . The search for Yage has failed. The mysterious Doctor Cotter wants only to be rid of his unwelcome guests. He suspects them to be agents of his treacherous partner Gill, intent on stealing his genius work of isolating curare from the composite arrow poison. I heard later that the chemical companies decided simply to buy up the arrow poison in quantity and extract the curare in their American laboratories. The drug was soon synthesized, and is now a standard substance found in many muscle-relaxing preparations. So it would seem that Cotter really had nothing to lose: his efforts were already superseded.

Dead end. And Puyo can serve as a model for the Place of Dead Roads: a dead, meaningless conglomerate of tin-roofed houses under a continual downpour of rain. Shell has pulled out, leaving prefabricated bungalows and rusting machinery behind. And Lee has reached the end of his line, an end implicit in the beginning. He is left with the impact of unbridgeable distances, the defeat and weariness of a long, painful journey made for nothing, wrong turnings, the track lost, a bus waiting in the rain . . . back to Ambato, Quito, Panama, Mexico City.

When I started to write this companion text to *Queer*, I was paralysed with a heavy reluctance, a writer's block like a straitjacket: 'I glance at the manuscript of *Queer* and feel I simply can't read it. My past was a poisoned river from which one was fortunate to escape, and by which one feels immediately threatened, years after the events recorded. – Painful to an extent I find it difficult to read, let alone to write about. Every word and gesture sets the teeth on edge.' The reason for this reluctance becomes clearer as I force myself to look: the book is motivated and formed by an event which is never mentioned, in fact is carefully avoided: the accidental shooting death of my wife, Joan, in September 1951.

While I was writing *The Place of Dead Roads*, I felt in spiritual contact with the late English writer Denton

Welch, and modelled the novel's hero, Kim Carson, directly on him. Whole sections came to me as if dictated, like table-tapping. I have written about the fateful morning of Denton's accident, which left him an invalid for the remainder of his short life. If he had stayed a little longer here, not so long there, he would have missed his appointment with the female motorist who hit his bicycle from behind for no apparent reason. At one point Denton had stopped to have coffee, and looking at the brass hinges on the café's window shutters, some of them broken, he was hit by a feeling of universal desolation and loss. So every event of that morning is charged with special significance, as if it were <u>underlined</u>. This portentous second sight permeates Welch's writing: a scone, a cup of tea, an inkwell purchased for a few shillings, become charged with a special and often sinister significance.

I get exactly the same feeling to an almost unbearable degree as I read the manuscript of *Queer*. The event towards which Lee feels himself inexorably driven is the death of his wife by his own hand, the knowledge of possession, a dead hand waiting to slip over his like a glove. So a smog of menace and evil rises from the pages, an evil that Lee, knowing and yet not knowing, tries to escape with frantic flights of fantasy: his routines, which set one's teeth on edge because of the ugly menace just behind or to one side of them, a presence palpable as a haze.

Brion Gysin said to me in Paris: 'For ugly spirit shot Joan because . . .' A bit of mediumistic message that was not completed – or was it? It doesn't need to be completed, if you read it: 'ugly spirit shot Joan *to be cause*,' that is, to maintain a hateful parasitic occupation. My concept of possession is closer to the medieval model than to modern psychological explanations, with their dogmatic insistence that such manifestations must come from within and never, never, never from without. (As if there were some clear-cut difference between inner and outer.) I mean a definite possessing entity. And indeed, the psychological concept might well have been devised by the possessing entities, since nothing is more dangerous to a possessor than being seen as a separate invading creature by the host it has invaded. And for this reason the possessor shows itself only when absolutely necessary.

In 1939, I became interested in Egyptian hieroglyphics and went out to see someone in the Department of Egyptology at the University of Chicago. And something was screaming in my ear: 'YOU DON'T BELONG HERE!' Yes, the hieroglyphics provided one key to the mechanism of possession. Like a virus, the possessing entity must find a port of entry.

This occasion was my first clear indication of something in my being that was not me, and not under my control. I remember a dream from this period: I worked as an exterminator in Chicago, in the late 1930s, and lived in a rooming house on the near North Side. In the dream I am floating up near the ceiling with a feeling of utter death and despair, and looking down I see my body walking out the door with deadly purpose.

One wonders if Yage could have saved the day by a blinding revelation. I remember a cut-up I made in Paris years later: 'Raw peeled winds of hate and mischance blew the shot.' And for years I thought this referred to blowing a shot of junk, when the junk squirts out the side of the syringe or dropper owing to an obstruction. Brion Gysin pointed out the actual meaning: the shot that killed Joan.

*

I had bought a Scout knife in Quito. It had a metal handle and a curious tarnished old look, like something from a turn-of-the-century junk shop. I can see it in a tray of old knives and rings, with the silver plate flaking off. It was about three o'clock in the afternoon, a few days after I came back to Mexico City, and I decided to have the knife sharpened. The knife-sharpener had a little whistle and a fixed route, and as I walked down the street towards his cart a feeling of loss and sadness that had weighed on me all day so I could hardly breathe intensified to such an extent that I found tears streaming down my face.

'What on earth is wrong?' I wondered.

This heavy depression and a feeling of doom occurs again and again in the text. Lee usually attributes it to his failures with Allerton: 'A heavy drag slowed movement and thought. Lee's face was rigid, his voice toneless.' Allerton has just refused a dinner invitation and left abruptly: 'Lee stared at the table, his thoughts slow, as if he were very cold.' (Reading this *I am* cold and depressed.)

Here is a precognitive dream from Cotter's shack in Ecuador: 'He was standing in front of the Ship Ahoy. The place looked deserted. He could hear someone crying. He saw his little son, and knelt down and took the child in his arms. The sound of crying came closer, a wave of sadness . . . He held little Willy close against his chest. A group of people were standing there in convict suits. Lee wondered what they were doing there and why he was crying.'

I have constrained myself to remember the day of Joan's death, the overwhelming feeling of doom and loss . . . walking down the street I suddenly found tears streaming down my face. 'What is wrong with me?' The small Scout knife with a metal handle, the plating peeling off, a smell of old coins, the knife-sharpener's whistle. Whatever happened to this knife I never reclaimed?

I am forced to the appalling conclusion that I would never have become a writer but for Joan's death, and to a realization of the extent to which this event has motivated and formulated my writing. I live with the constant threat of possession, and a constant need to escape from possession, from Control. So the death of Joan brought me in contact with the invader, the Ugly Spirit, and maneuvered me into a lifelong struggle, in which I have had no choice except to write my way out.

I have constrained myself to escape death. Denton Welch is almost my face. Smell of old coins. Whatever happened to this knife called Allerton, back to the appalling Margaras Inc. The realization is basic formulated **doing***? The day of Joan's doom and loss. Found tears streaming down from Allerton peeling off the same person as a Western shootist.* **What are you rewriting?** *A lifelong preoccupation with Control and Virus. Having gained access the virus uses the host's energy, blood, flesh and bones to make copies of itself. Model of dogmatic insistence never from without was screaming in my ear, 'YOU DON'T BELONG HERE!'*

A straitjacket notation carefully paralysed with heavy reluctance. To escape their prewritten lines years after the events recorded. A writer's block avoided Joan's death. Denton Welch is Kim Carson's voice through a cloud underlined broken table tapping.

William S. Burroughs
February 1985

Queer

Chapter 1

Lee turned his attention to a Jewish boy named Carl Steinberg, whom he had known casually for about a year. The first time he saw Carl, Lee thought, 'I could use that, if the family jewels weren't in pawn to Uncle Junk.'

The boy was blond, his face thin and sharp with a few freckles, always a little pink around the ears and nose as though he had just washed. Lee had never known anyone to look as clean as Carl. With his small round brown eyes and fuzzy blond hair, he reminded Lee of a young bird. Born in Munich, Carl had grown up in Baltimore. In manner and outlook he seemed European. He shook hands with traces of a heel-click. In general, Lee found European youths easier to talk to than Americans. The rudeness of many Americans depressed him, a rudeness based on a solid ignorance of the whole concept of manners, and on the proposition that for social purposes, all people are more or less equal and interchangeable.

What Lee looked for in any relationship was the feel of contact. He felt some contact with Carl. The boy listened politely and seemed to understand what Lee was saying. After some initial balking, he accepted the fact of Lee's sexual interest in his person. He told Lee, 'Since I can't change my mind about you, I will have to change my mind about other things.'

But Lee soon found out he could make no progress. 'If I got this far with an American kid,' he reasoned, 'I could get the rest of the way. So he's not queer. People can be obliging. What is the obstacle?' Lee finally guessed the answer: 'What makes it impossible is that his mother wouldn't like it.' And Lee knew it was time to pack in. He recalled a homosexual Jewish friend who lived in Oklahoma City. Lee had asked, 'Why do you live here? You have enough money to live anywhere you like.' The reply was, 'It would kill my mother if I moved away.' Lee had been speechless.

One afternoon Lee was walking with Carl by the Amsterdam Avenue park. Suddenly Carl bowed slightly and shook Lee's hand. 'Best of luck,' he said, and ran for a streetcar.

Lee stood looking after him, then walked over into the park and sat down on a concrete bench that was molded to resemble wood. Blue flowers from a blossoming tree had fallen on the bench and on the walk in front of it. Lee sat there watching the flowers move along the path in a warm spring wind. The sky was clouding up for an afternoon shower. Lee felt lonely and defeated. 'I'll have to look for someone else,' he thought. He covered his face with his hands. He was very tired.

He saw a shadowy line of boys. As each boy came to the front of the line, he said 'Best of luck,' and ran for a streetcar.

'Sorry . . . wrong number . . . try again . . . somewhere else . . . someplace else . . . not here . . . not me . . . can't use it, don't need it, don't want it. Why pick on me?' The last face was so real and so ugly, Lee said aloud, 'Who asked you, you ugly son of a bitch?'

Lee opened his eyes and looked around. Two Mexican adolescents walked by, their arms around each other's necks. He looked after them, licking his dry, cracked lips.

Lee continued to see Carl after that, until finally Carl said 'Best of luck' for the last time, and walked away. Lee heard later he had gone with his family to Uruguay.

Lee was sitting with Winston Moor in the Rathskeller, drinking double tequilas. Cuckoo clocks and moth-eaten deer heads gave the restaurant a dreary, out-of-place, Tyrolean look. A smell of spilt beer, overflowing toilets and sour garbage hung in the place like a thick fog and drifted out into the street through narrow, inconvenient swinging doors. A television set which was out of order half the time and which emitted horrible, guttural squawks was the final touch of unpleasantness.

'I was in here last night,' Lee said to Moor. 'Got talking to a queer doctor and his boyfriend. The doctor was a major in the Medical Corps. The boy-friend is some kind of vague engineer. Awful-looking little bitch. So the doctor invites me to have a drink with them, and the boyfriend is getting jealous, and I don't want a beer anyway, which the doctor takes as a reflection on Mexico and on his own person. He begins the do-you-like Mexico routine. So I tell him Mexico is okay, some of it, but he personally is a pain in the ass. Told him this in a nice way, you understand. Besides, I had to go home to my wife in any case.

'So he says, "You don't have any wife, you are just as

queer as I am." I told him, "I don't know how queer you are, Doc, and I ain't about to find out. It isn't as if you was a good-looking Mexican. You're a goddamned old ugly-looking Mexican. And that goes double for your moth-eaten boyfriend." I was hoping, of course, the deal wouldn't come to any extreme climax . . .

"You never knew Hatfield? Of course not. Before your time. He killed a *cargador* in a *pulquería*. The deal cost him five hundred dollars. Now, figuring a *cargador* as rock bottom, think how much it would cost you to shoot a major in the Mexican Army.'

Moor called the waiter over. 'Yo quiero un sandwich,' he said, smiling at the waiter. "¿Quel sandwiches tiene?'

'What do you want?' Lee asked, annoyed at the interruption.

'I don't know exactly,' said Moor, looking through the menu. 'I wonder if they could make a melted cheese sandwich on toasted whole-wheat bread?' Moor turned back to the waiter, with a smile that was intended to be boyish.

Lee closed his eyes as Moor launched an attempt to convey the concept of melted cheese on wholewheat toast. Moor was being charmingly helpless with his inadequate Spanish. He was putting down a little-boy-in-a-foreign-country routine. Moor smiled into an inner mirror, a smile without a trace of warmth, but it was not a cold smile: it was the meaningless smile of senile decay, the smile that goes with false teeth, the smile of a man grown old and stir-simple in the solitary confinement of exclusive self-love.

Moor was a thin young man with blond hair that was habitually somewhat long. He had pale blue eyes and very white skin. There were dark patches under his eyes and two deep lines around the mouth. He looked like a child, and at the same time like a prematurely aged man. His face showed the ravages of the death process, the inroads of decay in flesh cut off from the living charge of contact. Moor was motivated, literally kept alive and moving, by hate, but there was no passion or violence in his hate. Moor's hate was a slow, steady push, weak but infinitely persistent, waiting to take advantage of any weakness in another. The slow drip of Moor's hate had etched the lines of decay in his face. He had aged without experience of life, like a piece of meat rotting on a pantry shelf.

Moor made a practice of interrupting a story just before the point was reached. Often he would start a long conversation with a waiter or anybody else handy, or he would go vague and distant, yawn, and say, 'What was that?' as though recalled to dull reality from reflections of which others could have no concept.

Moor began talking about his wife. 'At first, Bill, she was so dependent on me that she used literally to have hysterics when I had to go to the museum where I work. I managed to build up her ego to the point where she didn't need me, and after that the only thing I could do was leave. There was nothing more I could do for her.'

Moor was putting down his sincere act. 'My God,' Lee thought, 'he really believes it.'

Lee ordered another double tequila. Moor stood up. 'Well, I have to get going,' he said. 'I have a lot of things to do.'

'Well, listen,' said Lee. 'How about dinner tonight?'

Moor said, 'Well, all right.'

'At six in the K.C. Steak House.'

'All right.' Moor left.

Lee drank half the tequila the waiter put in front of him. He had known Moor off and on in N.Y. for several years and never liked him. Moor disliked Lee, but then Moor didn't like anybody. Lee told himself, 'You must be crazy, making passes in that direction, when you know what a bitch he is. These borderline characters can out-bitch any fag.'

When Lee arrived at the K.C. Steak House, Moor was already there. With him he had Tom Williams, another Salt Lake City boy. Lee thought, 'He brought along a chaperone.'

'. . . I like the guy, Tom, but I can't stand to be alone with him. He keeps trying to go to bed with me. That's what I don't like about queers. You can't keep it on a basis of friendship . . .' Yes, Lee could hear that conversation.

During dinner Moor and Williams talked about a boat they planned to build at Ziuhuatenejo. Lee thought this was a silly project. 'Boat building is a job for a professional, isn't it?' Lee asked. Moor pretended not to hear.

After dinner Lee walked back to Moor's rooming house with Moor and Williams. At the door Lee asked, 'Would you gentlemen care for a drink? I'll get a bottle . . .' He looked from one to the other.

Moor said, 'Well, no. You see we want to work on the plans for this boat we are going to build.'

'Oh,' said Lee. 'Well, I'll see you tomorrow. How about meeting me for a drink in the Rathskeller? Say around five.'

'Well, I expect I'll be busy tomorrow.'

'Yes, but you have to eat and drink.'

'Well, you see, this boat is more important to me than anything right now. It will take up all my time.'

Lee said, 'Suit yourself,' and walked away.

Lee was deeply hurt. He could hear Moor saying, 'Thanks for running interference, Tom. Well, I hope he got the idea. Of course Lee is an interesting guy and all that . . . but this queer situation is just more than I can take.' Tolerant, looking at both sides of the question, sympathetic up to a point, finally forced to draw a tactful but firm line. 'And he really believes that,' Lee thought. 'Like that crap about building up his wife's ego. He can revel in the satisfactions of virulent bitchiness and simultaneously see himself as a saint. Quite a trick.'

Actually Moor's brush-off was calculated to inflict the maximum hurt possible under the circumstances. It put Lee in the position of a detestably insistent queer, too stupid and too insensitive to realize that his attentions were not wanted, forcing Moor to the distasteful necessity of drawing a diagram.

Lee leaned against a lamppost for several minutes. The shock had sobered him, drained away his drunken euphoria. He realized how tired he was, and how weak, but he was not ready yet to go home.

Chapter 2

'Everything made in this country falls apart,' Lee thought. He was examining the blade of his stainless-steel pocketknife. The chrome plating was peeling off like silver paper. 'Wouldn't surprise me if I picked up a boy in the Alameda and his ... Here comes honest Joe.'

Joe Guidry sat down at the table with Lee, dropping bundles on the table and in the empty chair. He wiped off the top of a beer bottle with his sleeve and drank half the beer in a long gulp. He was a large man with a politician's red Irish face.

'What you know?' Lee asked.

'Not much, Lee. Except someone stole my typewriter. And I know who took it. It was that Brazilian, or whatever he is. You know him. Maurice.'

'Maurice? Is that the one you had last week? The wrestler?'

'You mean Louie, the gym instructor. No, this is another one. Louie has decided all that sort of thing is very wrong and he tells me that I am going to burn in hell, but *he* is going to heaven.'

'Serious?'

'Oh, yes. Well, Maurice is as queer as I am.' Joe

belched. 'Excuse me. If not queerer. But he won't accept it. I think stealing my typewriter is a way he takes to demonstrate to me and to himself that he is just in it for all he can get. As a matter of fact, he's so queer I've lost interest in him. Not completely though. When I see the little bastard I'll most likely invite him back to my apartment, instead of beating the shit out of him like I should.'

Lee tipped his chair back against the wall and looked around the room. Someone was writing a letter at the next table. If he had overheard the conversation, he gave no sign. The proprietor was reading the bull-fight section of the paper, spread out on the counter in front of him. A silence peculiar to Mexico seeped into the room, a vibrating, soundless hum.

Joe finished his beer, wiped his mouth with the back of his hand, and stared at the wall with watery, blood-shot blue eyes. The silence seeped into Lee's body, and his face went slack and blank. The effect was curiously spectral, as though you could see though his face. The face was ravaged and vicious and old, but the clear, green eyes were dreamy and innocent. His light-brown hair was extremely fine and would not stay combed. Generally it fell down across his forehead, and on occasion brushed the food he was eating or got in his drink.

'Well, I have to be going,' said Joe. He gathered up his bundles and nodded to Lee, bestowing on him one of his sweet politician smiles, and walked out, his fuzzy, half-bald head outlined for a moment in the sunlight before he disappeared from view.

Lee yawned and picked up a comic section from the next table. It was two days old. He put it down and yawned again. He got up and paid for his drink and walked out into the late afternoon sun. He had no place to go, so he went over to Sears' magazine counter and read the new magazines for free.

He cut back past the K.C. Steak House. Moor beckoned to him from inside the restaurant. Lee went in and sat down at his table. 'You look terrible,' he said. He knew that was what Moor wanted to hear. As a matter of fact, Moor did look worse than usual. He had always been pale: now he was yellowish.

The boat project had fallen through. Moor and Williams and Williams' wife, Lil, were back from Ziuhuatenejo. Moor was not on speaking terms with the Williamses.

Lee ordered a pot of tea. Moor started talking about Lil. 'You know, Lil ate the cheese down there. She ate everything and she never got sick. She won't go to a doctor. One morning she woke up blind in one eye and she could barely see out the other. But she wouldn't have a doctor. In a few days she could see again, good as ever. I was hoping she'd go blind.'

Lee realized Moor was perfectly serious. 'He's insane,' Lee thought.

Moor went on about Lil. She had made advances to him, of course. He had paid more than his share of the rent and food. She was a terrible cook. They had left him there sick. He shifted to the subject of his health. 'Just let me show you my urine test,' Moor said with boyish enthusiasm. He spread the piece of paper out on the table. Lee looked at it without interest.

'Look here.' Moor pointed. 'Urea thirteen. Normal is fifteen to twenty-two. Is that serious, do you think?'

'I'm sure I don't know.'

'And traces of sugar. What does the whole picture mean?' Moor obviously considered the question of intense interest.

'Why don't you take it to a doctor?'

'I did. He said he would have to take a twenty-four-hour test, that is, samples of urine over a twenty-four-hour period, before he could express any opinion . . . You know, I have a dull pain in the chest, right here. I wonder if it could be tuberculosis?'

'Take an x-ray.'

'I did. The doctor is going to take a skin reaction test. Oh, another thing, I think I have undulant fever . . . Do you think I have fever now?' He pushed his forehead forward for Lee to feel. Lee felt an ear lobe. 'I don't think so,' he said.

Moor went on and on, following the circular route of the true hypochondriac, back to tuberculosis and the urine test. Lee thought he had never heard anything as tiresome and depressing. Moor did not have tuberculosis or kidney trouble or undulant fever. He was sick with the sickness of death. Death was in every cell of his body. He gave off a faint, greenish steam of decay. Lee imagined he would glow in the dark.

Moor talked with boyish eagerness. 'I think I need an operation.'

Lee said he really had to go.

Lee turned down Coahuila, walking with one foot falling directly in front of the other, always fast and purposeful, as if he were leaving the scene of a holdup. He passed a group in expatriate uniform: red-checked shirt outside the belt, blue jeans and beard, and another group of young men in conventional, if shabby, clothes. Among these Lee recognized a boy named Eugene Allerton. Allerton was tall and very thin, with high cheekbones, a small, bright-red mouth, and amber-colored eyes that took on a faint violet flush when he was drunk. His gold-brown hair was differentially bleached by the sun like a sloppy dyeing job. He had straight, black eyebrows and black eyelashes. An equivocal face, very young, clean-cut and boyish, at the same time conveying an impression of make-up, delicate and exotic and Oriental. Allerton was never completely neat or clean, but you did not think of him as being dirty. He was simply careless and lazy to the point of appearing, at times, only half awake. Often he did not hear what someone said a foot from his ear. 'Pallagra, I expect,' thought Lee sourly. He nodded to Allerton and smiled. Allerton nodded, as if surprised, and did not smile.

Lee walked on, a little depressed. 'Perhaps I can accomplish something in that direction. Well, *a ver . . .*' He froze in front of a restaurant like a bird dog: 'Hungry . . . quicker to eat here than buy something and cook it.' When Lee was hungry, when he wanted a drink or a shot of morphine, delay was unbearable.

He went in, ordered steak *a la Mexicana* and a glass of milk, and waited with his mouth watering for food. A young man with a round face and a loose mouth came into the restaurant. Lee said, 'Hello, Horace,' in a clear voice. Horace nodded without speaking and sat down as far from Lee as he could get in the small restaurant. Lee smiled. His food arrived and he ate quickly, like an animal, cramming bread and steak into his mouth and washing it down with gulps of milk. He leaned back in his chair and lit a cigarette.

'*Un café sólo*,' he called to the waitress as she walked by, carrying a pineapple soda to two young Mexicans in double-breasted pinstripe suits. One of the Mexicans had moist brown pop-eyes and a scraggly moustache of greasy black hairs. He looked pointedly at Lee, and Lee looked away. 'Careful,' he thought, 'or he will be over here asking me how I like Mexico.' He dropped his half-smoked cigarette into half an inch of cold coffee, walked over to the counter, paid the bill, and was out of the restaurant before the Mexican could formulate an opening sentence. When Lee decided to leave some place, his departure was abrupt.

The Ship Ahoy had a few phony hurricane lamps by way of a nautical atmosphere. Two small rooms with tables, the bar in one room, and four high, precarious stools. The place was always dimly lit and sinister-looking. The patrons were tolerant, but in no way bohemian. The bearded set never frequented the Ship Ahoy. The place existed on borrowed time, without a liquor license, under many changes of management. At this time it was run by an American named Tom Weston and an American-born Mexican.

Lee walked directly to the bar and ordered a drink. He drank it and ordered a second one before looking around the room to see if Allerton was there. Allerton was alone at a table, tipped back in a chair with one leg crossed over the other, holding a bottle of beer on his knee. He nodded to Lee. Lee tried to achieve a greeting at once friendly and casual, designed to show interest without pushing their short acquaintance. The result was ghastly.

As Lee stood aside to bow in his dignified old-world greeting, there emerged instead a leer of naked lust, wrenched in the pain and hate of his deprived body and, in simultaneous double exposure, a sweet child's smile of liking and trust, shockingly out of time and out of place, mutilated and hopeless.

Allerton was appalled. 'Perhaps he has some sort of

tic,' he thought. He decided to remove himself from contact with Lee before the man did something even more distasteful. The effect was like a broken connection. Allerton was not cold or hostile; Lee simply wasn't there so far as he was concerned. Lee looked at him helplessly for a moment, then turned back to the bar, defeated and shaken.

Lee finished his second drink. When he looked around again, Allerton was playing chess with Mary, an American girl with dyed red hair and carefully applied make-up, who had come into the bar in the meantime. 'Why waste time here?' Lee thought. He paid for the two drinks and walked out.

He took a cab to the Chimu Bar, which was a fag bar frequented by Mexicans, and spent the night with a young boy he met there.

At that time the G.I. students patronized Lola's during the daytime and the Ship Ahoy at night. Lola's was not exactly a bar. It was a small beer-and-soda joint. There was a Coca-Cola box full of beer and soda and ice at the left of the door as you came in. A counter with tube-metal stools covered in yellow glazed leather ran down one side of the room as far as the juke box. Tables were lined along the wall opposite the counter. The stools had long since lost the rubber caps for the legs, and made horrible screeching noises when the maid pushed them around to sweep. There was a kitchen in back, where a slovenly cook fried everything in rancid fat. There was neither past nor future in Lola's. The place was a waiting room, where certain people checked in at certain times.

Several days after his pick-up in the Chimu, Lee was

sitting in Lola's, reading aloud from *Últimas Notícias* to Jim Cochan. There was a story about a man who murdered his wife and children. Cochan looked about for means to escape, but every time he made a move to go, Lee pinned him down with: 'Get a load of this . . . "When his wife came home from the market, her husband, already drunk, was brandishing his .45." Why do they always have to brandish it?'

Lee read to himself for a moment. Cochan stirred uneasily. 'Jesus Christ,' said Lee, looking up. 'After he killed his wife and three children he takes a razor and puts on a suicide act.' He turned to the paper: '"But resulted only with scratches that did not require medical attention." What a slobbish performance!' He turned the page and began reading the leads half-aloud: 'They're cutting the butter with Vaseline. Fine thing. Lobster with drawn K.Y. . . Here's a man was surprised in his taco stand with a dressed-down dog . . . a great long skinny hound dog at that. There's a picture of him posing in front of his taco stand with the dog . . . One citizen asked another for a light. The party in second part don't have a match so first part pulls an ice pick and kills him. Murder is the national neurosis of Mexico.'

Cochan stood up. Lee was on his feet instantly. 'Sit down on your ass, or what's left of it after four years in the Navy,' he said.

'I got to go.'

'What are you, henpecked?'

'No kidding. I been out too much lately. My old lady . . .'

Lee wasn't listening. He had just seen Allerton stroll by outside the door and look in. Allerton had not greeted Lee, but walked on after a momentary pause. 'I was in the shadow,' Lee thought. 'He couldn't see me from the door.' Lee did not notice Cochan's departure.

On a sudden impulse he rushed out the door. Allerton was half a block away. Lee overtook him. Allerton turned, raising his eyebrows, which were straight and black as a pen stroke. He looked surprised and a bit alarmed, since he was dubious of Lee's sanity. Lee improvised desperately.

'I just wanted to tell you Mary was in Lola's a little while ago. She asked me to tell you she would be in the Ship Ahoy later on, around five.' This was partly true. Mary had been in and had asked Lee if he had seen Allerton.

Allerton was relieved. 'Oh, thank you,' he said, quite cordial now. 'Will you be around tonight?'

'Yes, I think so.' Lee nodded and smiled, and turned away quickly.

Lee left his apartment for the Ship Ahoy just before five. Allerton was sitting at the bar. Lee sat down and ordered a drink, then turned to Allerton with a casual greeting, as though they were on familiar and friendly terms. Allerton returned the greeting automatically before he realized that Lee had somehow established himself on a familiar basis, whereas he had previously decided to have as little to do with Lee as possible. Allerton had a talent for ignoring people, but he was not competent at dislodging someone from a position already occupied.

Lee began talking – casual, unpretentiously intelligently, dryly humorous. Slowly he dispelled Allerton's impression that he was a peculiar and undesirable character. When Mary arrived, Lee greeted her with a tipsy old-world gallantry and, excusing himself, left them to a game of chess.

'Who is he?' asked Mary when Lee had gone outside.

'I have no idea,' said Allerton. Had he ever met Lee? He could not be sure. Formal introductions were not expected among the G.I. students. Was Lee a student? Allerton had never seen him at the school. There was nothing unusual in talking to someone you didn't know, but Lee put Allerton on guard. The man was somehow familiar to him. When Lee talked, he seemed to mean more than what he said. A special emphasis to a word or a greeting hinted at a period of familiarity in some other time and place. As though Lee were saying,'*You* know what I mean. *You* remember.'

Allerton shrugged irritably and began arranging the chess pieces on the board. He looked like a sullen child unable to locate the source of his ill temper. After a few minutes of play his customary serenity returned, and he began humming.

It was after midnight when Lee returned to the Ship Ahoy. Drunks seethed around the bar, talking as if everyone else were stone deaf. Allerton stood on the edge of this group, apparently unable to make himself heard. He greeted Lee warmly, pushed in to the bar, and emerged with two rum Cokes. 'Let's sit down over here,' he said.

Allerton was drunk. His eyes were flushed a faint violet tinge, the pupils widely dilated. He was talking very fast in a high, thin voice, the eerie, disembodied voice of a young child. Lee had never heard Allerton talk like this before. The effect was like the possession voice of a medium. The boy had an inhuman gaiety and innocence.

Allerton was telling a story about his experience with the Counter-Intelligence Corps in Germany. An informant had been giving the department bum steers.

'How did you check the accuracy of information?' Lee asked. 'How did you know ninety percent of what your informants told you wasn't fabricated?'

'Actually we didn't, and we got sucked in on a lot of phony deals. Of course, we cross-checked all information with other informants and we had our own agents in the field. Most of our informants turned in *some* phony information, but this one character made all of it up. He had our agents out looking for a whole fictitious network of Russian spies. So finally the report comes back from Frankfurt – it is all a lot of crap. But instead of clearing out of town before the information could be checked, he came back with more.

'At this point we'd really had enough of his bullshit. So we locked him up in a cellar. The room was pretty cold and uncomfortable, but that was all we could do. We had to handle prisoners very careful. He kept typing out confessions, enormous things.'

This story clearly delighted Allerton, and he kept laughing while he was telling it. Lee was impressed by his combination of intelligence and childlike charm. Allerton was friendly now, without reserve or defense, like a child who has never been hurt. He was telling another story.

Lee watched the thin hands, the beautiful violet eyes, the flush of excitement on the boy's face. An imaginary hand projected with such force it seemed Allerton must feel the touch of ectoplasmic fingers caressing his ear, phantom thumbs smoothing his eyebrows, pushing the hair back from his face. Now Lee's hands were running down over the ribs, the stomach. Lee felt the aching pain of desire in his lungs. His mouth was a little open, showing his teeth in the half-snarl of a baffled animal. He licked his lips.

Lee did not enjoy frustration. The limitations of his desires were like the bars of a cage, like a chain and collar, something he had learned as an animal learns, through days and years of experiencing the snubs of the chain, the unyielding bars. He had never resigned himself, and his eyes looked out through the invisible bars, watchful, alert, waiting for the keeper to forget the door, for the frayed collar, the loosened bar . . . suffering without despair and without consent.

'I went to the door and there he was with a branch in his mouth,' Allerton was saying.

Lee had not been listening. 'A branch in his mouth,' said Lee, then added inanely, 'A big branch?'

'It was about two feet long. I told him to drop dead, then a few minutes later he appeared at the window. So I threw a chair at him and he jumped down to the yard from the balcony. About eighteen feet. He was very nimble. Almost inhuman. It was sort of uncanny, and that's why I threw the chair. I was scared. We all figured he was putting on an act to get out of the Army.'

'What did he look like?' Lee asked.

'Look like? I don't remember especially. He was around eighteen. He looked like a clean-cut boy. We threw a bucket of cold water on him and left him on a cot downstairs. He began flopping around but he didn't say anything. We all decided that was an appropriate punishment. I think they took him to the hospital next day.'

'Pneumonia?'

'I don't know. Maybe we shouldn't have thrown water on him.'

Lee left Allerton at the door of his building.

'You go in here?' Lee asked.

'Yes, I have a sack here.'

Lee said good night and walked home.

After that, Lee met Allerton every day at five in the Ship Ahoy. Allerton was accustomed to choose his friends from people older than himself, and he looked forward to meeting Lee. Lee had conversational routines that Allerton had never heard. But he felt at times oppressed by Lee, as though Lee's presence shut off everything else. He thought he was seeing too much of Lee.

Allerton disliked commitments, and had never been in love or had a close friend. He was now forced to ask himself: 'What does he want from me?' It did not occur to him that Lee was queer, as he associated queerness with at least some degree of overt effeminacy. He decided finally that Lee valued him as an audience.

Chapter 3

It was a beautiful, clear afternoon in April. Punctually at five, Lee walked into the Ship Ahoy. Allerton was at the bar with Al Hyman, a periodic alcoholic and one of the nastiest, stupidest, dullest drunks Lee had ever known. He was, on the other hand, intelligent and simple in manner, and nice enough when sober. He was sober now.

Lee had a yellow scarf around his neck, and a pair of two-peso sunglasses. He took off the scarf and dark glasses and dropped them on the bar. 'A hard day at the studio,' he said, in affected theatrical accents. He ordered a rum Coke. 'You know, it looks like we might bring in an oil well. They're drilling now over in quadrangle four, and from that rig you could almost spit over into Tex-Mex where I got my hundred-acre cotton farm.'

'I always wanted to be an oilman,' Hyman said.

Lee looked him over and shook his head. 'I'm afraid not. You see, it isn't everybody can qualify. You must have the calling. First thing, you must look like an oilman. There are no young oilmen. An oilman should be about fifty. His skin is cracked and wrinkled like mud that has dried in the sun, and especially the back of his neck is wrinkled, and the wrinkles are generally full of dust from looking over blocks and quadrangles. He wears gabardine slacks and a white short-sleeved sport shirt. His shoes are covered with fine dust, and a faint haze of dust follows him everywhere like a personal dust storm.

'So you got the calling and the proper appearance. You go around taking up leases. You get five or six people lined up to lease you their land for drilling. You go to the bank and talk to the president: "Now Clem Farris, as fine a man as there is in this Valley and smart too, he's in this thing up to his balls, and Old Man Scranton and Fred Crockly and Roy Spigot and Ted Bane, all of them good old boys. Now let me show you a few facts. I could set here and gas all morning, taking up your time, but I know you're a man accustomed to deal in facts and figures and that's exactly what I'm here to show you."

'He goes out to his car, always a coupé or a roadster – never saw an oilman with a sedan – and reaches in back of the seat and gets out his maps, a huge bundle of maps as big as carpets. He spreads them out on the bank president's desk, and great clouds of dust spring up from the maps and fill the bank.

'"You see this quadrangle here? That's Tex-Mex. Now there's a fault runs right along here through Jed Marvin's place. I saw Old Jed too, the other day when I was out there, a good old boy. There isn't a finer man in this Valley than Jed Marvin. Well now, Socony drilled right over here."

'He spreads out more maps. He pulls over another desk and anchors the maps down with cuspidors. "Well, they brought in a dry hole, and this map . . ." He unrolls another one. "Now if you'll kindly sit on the other end so it don't roll up on us, I'll show you exactly why it was a dry hole and why they should never have drilled there in the first place, 'cause you can see just where this here fault runs smack between Jed's artesian well and the Tex-Mex line over into quadrangle four. Now that block was surveyed last time in 1922. I guess you know the old boy done the job. Earl Hoot was his name, a good old boy too. He had his home up in Nacogdoches, but his son-in-law owned a place down here, the old Brooks place up north of Tex-Mex, just across the line from . . ."

'By this time the president is punchy with boredom, and the dust is getting down in his lungs – oilmen are constitutionally immune to the effects of dust – so he says, "Well, if it's good enough for those boys I guess it's good enough for me. I'll go along."

'So the oilman goes back and pulls the same routine on his prospects. Then he gets a geologist down from Dallas or somewhere, who talks some gibberish about faults and seepage and intrusions and shale and sand, and selects some place, more or less at random, to start drilling.

'Now the driller. He has to be a real rip-snorting character. They look for him in Boy's Town – the whore district in border towns – and they find him in a room full of empty bottles with three whores. So they bust a bottle over his head and drag him out and sober him up, and he looks at the drilling site and spits and says, "Well, it's your hole."

'Now if the well turns out dry the oilman says, "Well, that's the way it goes. Some holes got lubrication, and some is dry as a whore's cunt on Sunday morning." There was one oilman, Dry Hole Dutton they called him – all right, Allerton, no cracks about Vaseline – brought in twenty dry holes before he got cured. That means "get rich", in the salty lingo of the oil fraternity.'

Joe Guidry came in, and Lee slid off his stool to shake hands. He was hoping Joe would bring up the subject of queerness so he could gauge Allerton's reaction. He figured it was time to let Allerton know what the score was – such a thing as playing it too cool.

They sat down at a table. Somebody had stolen Guidry's radio, his riding boots and wrist watch. 'The trouble with me is,' said Guidry, 'I like the type that robs me.'

'Where you make your mistake is bringing them to your apartment,' Lee said. 'That's what hotels are for.'

'You're right there. But half the time I don't have money for a hotel. Besides, I like someone around to cook breakfast and sweep the place out.'

'*Clean* the place out.'

'I don't mind the watch and the radio, but it really hurt, losing those boots. They were a thing of beauty and a joy forever.' Guidry leaned forward, and glanced at Allerton. 'I don't know whether I ought to say things like this in front of Junior here. No offense, kid.'

'Go ahead,' said Allerton.

'Did I tell you how I made the cop on the beat? He's the *vigilante*, the watchman out where I live. Every time he sees the light on in my room, he comes in for a shot of rum. Well, about five nights ago he caught me when I was drunk and horny, and one thing led to another and I ended up showing him how the cow ate the cabbage . . .

'So the night after I make him I was walking by the beer joint on the corner and he comes out *borracho* and says, "Have a drink." I said, "I don't want a drink." So he takes out his *pistola* and says, "Have a drink." I proceeded to take his *pistola* away from him, and he goes into the beer joint to phone for reinforcements.

So I had to go in and rip the phone off the wall. Now they're billing me for the phone. When I got back to my room, which is on the ground floor, he had written "*El Puto Gringo*" on the window with soap. So, instead of wiping it off, I left it there. It pays to advertise.'

The drinks kept coming. Allerton went to the W.C. and got in a conversation at the bar when he returned. Guidry was accusing Hyman of being queer and pretending not to be. Lee was trying to explain to Guidry that Hyman wasn't really queer, and Guidry said to him, 'He's queer and you aren't, Lee. You just go around pretending you're queer to get in on the act.'

'Who wants to get in on your tired old act?' Lee said. He saw Allerton at the bar talking to John Dumé. Dumé belonged to a small clique of queers who made their headquarters in a beer joint on Campeche called The Green Lantern. Dumé himself was not an obvious queer, but the other Green Lantern boys were screaming fags who would not have been welcome at the Ship Ahoy.

Lee walked over to the bar and started talking to the bartender. He thought, 'I hope Dumé tells him about me.' Lee felt uncomfortable in dramatic 'something-I-have-to-tell-you' routines and he knew, from unnerving experience, the difficulties of a casual come-on: 'I'm queer, you know, by the way.' Sometimes they don't hear right and yell, 'What?' Or you toss in: 'If you were as queer as I am.' The other yawns and changes the subject, and you don't know whether he understood or not.

The bartender was saying, 'She asks me why I drink. What can I tell her? I don't know why. Why did you have the monkey on your back? Do you know why? There isn't any why, but try to explain that to someone like Jerri. Try to explain that to any woman.' Lee nodded sympathetically. 'She says to me, why don't you get more sleep and eat better? She don't understand and I can't explain it. Nobody can explain it.'

The bartender moved away to wait on some customers. Dumé came over to Lee. 'How do you like this character?' he said, indicating Allerton with a wave of his beer bottle. Allerton was across the room talking to Mary and a chess player from Peru. 'He comes to me and says, "I thought you were one of the Green Lantern boys." So I said, "Well, I am." He wants me to take him around to some of the gay places here.'

Lee and Allerton went to see Cocteau's *Orpheus*. In the dark theater Lee could feel his body pull towards Allerton, an amoeboid protoplasmic projection, straining with a blind worm hunger to enter the other's body, to breathe with his lungs, see with his eyes, learn the feel of his viscera and genitals. Allerton shifted in his seat. Lee felt a sharp twinge, a strain or dislocation of the spirit. His eyes ached. He took off his glasses and ran his hand over his closed eyes.

When they left the theater, Lee felt exhausted. He fumbled and bumped into things. His voice was toneless with strain. He put his hand up to his head from time to time, and awkward, involuntary gesture of pain. 'I need a drink,' he said. he pointed to a bar across the street. 'There,' he said.

He sat down in a booth and ordered a double tequila. Allerton ordered rum and Coke. Lee drank the tequila straight down, listening down into himself for the effect. He ordered another.

'What did you think of the picture?' Lee asked.

'Enjoyed parts of it.'

'Yes.' Lee nodded, pursing his lips and looking down into his empty glass. 'So did I.' He pronounced the words very carefully, like an elocution teacher.

'He always gets some innaresting effects.' Lee laughed. Euphoria was spreading from his stomach. He drank half the second tequila. 'The innaresting thing about Cocteau is his ability to bring the myth alive in modern terms.'

'Ain't it the truth?' said Allerton.

They went to a Russian restaurant for dinner. Lee looked through the menu. 'By the way,' he said, 'the law was in putting the bite on the Ship Ahoy again. Vice squad. Two hundred pesos. I can see them in the station house after a hard day shaking down citizens of the Federal District. One cop says, "Ah, Gonzalez, you should see what I got today. Oh la la, such a bite!'

'"Aah, you shook down a *puto* queer for two *pesetas* in a bus station crapper. We know you, Hernandez, and your cheap tricks. You're the cheapest cop inna Federal District."'

Lee waved to the waiter. 'Hey, Jack. *Dos* martinis, much dry. *Seco*. And *dos* plates Sheeshka Babe. *Sabe?*'

The waiter nodded. 'That's two dry martinis and two orders of shish kebab. Right, gentlemen?'

'Solid, Pops ... So how was your evening with Dumé?'

'We went to several bars full of queers. One place a character asked me to dance and propositioned me.'

'Take him up?'

'No.'

'Dumé is a nice fellow.'

Allerton smiled. 'Yes, but he is not a person I would

49

confide too much in. That is, anything I wanted to keep private.'

'You refer to a specific indiscretion?'

'Frankly, yes.'

'I see.' Lee thought, 'Dumé never misses.'

The waiter put two martinis on the table. Lee held his martini up to the candle, looking at it with distaste. 'The inevitable watery martini with a decomposing olive,' he said.

Lee bought a lottery ticket from a boy of ten or so, who had rushed in when the waiter went to the kitchen. The boy was working the last-ticket routine. Lee paid him expansively, like a drunk American. 'Go buy yourself some marijuana, son,' he said. The boy smiled and turned to leave. 'Come back in five years and make an easy ten pesos,' Lee called after him.

Allerton smiled. 'Thank god,' Lee thought. 'I won't have to contend with middle-class morality.'

'Here you are, sir,' said the waiter, placing the shish kebab on the table.

Lee ordered two glasses of red wine. 'So Dumé told you about my, uh, proclivities?' he said abruptly.

'Yes,' said Allerton, his mouth full.

'A curse. Been in our family for generations. The Lees have always been perverts. I shall never forget the unspeakable horror that froze the lymph in my glands – the lymph glands that is, of course – when the baneful word seared my reeling brain: **I was a homosexual.** I thought of the painted, simpering female impersonators I had seen in a Baltimore night club. Could it be possible that I was one of those subhuman things? I walked the streets in a daze, like a man with a light concussion – just a minute, Doctor Kildare, this isn't your script. I might well have destroyed myself, ending an existence which seemed to offer nothing but grotesque misery and humiliation. Nobler, I thought, to die a man than live on, a sex monster. It was a wise old queen – Bobo, we called her – who taught me that I had a duty to live and to bear my burden proudly for all to see, to conquer prejudice and ignorance and hate with knowledge and sincerity and love. Whenever you are threatened by a hostile presence, you emit a thick cloud of love like an octopus squirts out ink . . .

'Poor Bobo came to a sticky end. He was riding in the Duc de Ventre's Hispano-Suiza when his falling piles blew out of the car and wrapped around the rear wheel. He was completely gutted, leaving an empty shell sitting there on the giraffe-skin upholstery. Even the eyes and the brain went, with a horrible shlupping sound. The Duc says he will carry that ghastly shlup with him to his mausoleum . . .

'Then I knew the meaning of loneliness. But Bobo's words came back to me from the tomb, the sibilants cracking gently. 'No one is every really alone. You are part of everything alive.' The difficulty is to convince someone else he is really part of you, so what the hell? Us parts ought to work together. Reet?'

Lee paused, looking at Allerton speculatively. 'Just where do I stand with the kid?' he wondered. He had listened politely, smiling at intervals. 'What I mean is, Allerton, we are all parts of a tremendous whole. No use fighting it.' Lee was getting tired of the routine. He looked around restlessly for some place to put it down. 'Don't these gay bars depress you? Of course, the queer bars here aren't to compare with Stateside queer joints.'

'I wouldn't know,' said Allerton. 'I've never been in any queer joints except those Dumé took me to. I guess there's kicks and kicks.'

'You haven't, really?'

'No, never.'

Lee paid the bill and they walked out into the cool night. A crescent moon was clear and green in the sky. They walked aimlessly.

'Shall we go to my place for a drink? I have some Napoleon brandy.'

'All right,' said Allerton.

'This is a completely unpretentious little brandy, you understand, none of this tourist treacle with obvious effects of flavoring, appealing to the mass tongue. My brandy has no need of shoddy devices to shock and coerce the palate. Come along.' Lee called a cab.

'Three pesos to Insurgentes and Monterrey,' Lee said to the driver in his atrocious Spanish. The driver said four. Lee waved him on. The driver muttered something, and opened the door.

Inside, Lee turned to Allerton. 'The man plainly harbors subversive thoughts. You know, when I was at Princeton, Communism was the thing. To come out flat for private and a class society, you marked yourself a stupid lout or suspect to be a High Episcopalian pederast. But I held out against the infection – of Communism I mean, of course.'

'*Aquí.*' Lee handed three pesos to the driver, who muttered some more and started the car with a vicious clash of gears.

'Sometimes I think they don't like us,' said Allerton.

'I don't mind people disliking me,' Lee said. 'The question is, what are they in a position to do about it? Apparently nothing, at present. They don't have the green light. This driver, for example, hates gringos. But if he kills someone – and very possibly he will – it will not be an American. It will be another Mexican. Maybe his good friend. Friends are less frightening than strangers.'

Lee opened the door of his apartment and turned on

the light. The apartment was pervaded by seemingly hopeless disorder. Here and there, ineffectual attempts had been made to arrange things in piles. There were no lived-in touches. No pictures, no decorations. Clearly, none of the furniture was his. But Lee's presence permeated the apartment. A coat over the back of a chair and a hat on the table were immediately recognizable as belonging to Lee.

'I'll fix you a drink.' Lee got two water glasses from the kitchen and poured two inches of Mexican brandy in each glass.

Allerton tasted the brandy. 'Good Lord,' he said. 'Napoleon must have pissed in this one.'

'I was afraid of that. An untutored palate. Your generation has never learned the pleasures that a trained palate confers on the disciplined few.'

Lee took a long drink of the brandy. He attempted an ecstatic 'aah', inhaled some of the brandy, and began to cough. 'It *is* god-awful,' he said when he could talk. 'Still, better than California brandy. It has a suggestion of cognac taste.'

There was a long silence. Allerton was sitting with his head leaning back against the couch. His eyes were half closed.

'Can I show you over the house?' said Lee, standing up. 'In here we have the bedroom.'

Allerton got to his feet slowly. They went into the bedroom, and Allerton lay down on the bed and lit a cigarette. Lee sat in the only chair.

'More brandy?' Lee asked. Allerton nodded. Lee sat down on the edge of the bed, and filled his glass and handed it to him. Lee touched his sweater. 'Sweet stuff, dearie,' he said. 'That wasn't made in Mexico.'

'I bought it in Scotland,' he said. He began to hiccough violently, and got up and rushed for the bathroom.

Lee stood in the doorway. 'Too bad,' he said. 'What could be the matter? You didn't drink much.' He filled a glass with water and handed it to Allerton. 'You all right now?' he asked.

'Yes, I think so.' Allerton lay down on the bed again.

Lee reached out a hand and touched Allerton's ear, and caressed the side of his face. Allerton reached up and covered one of Lee's hands and squeezed it.

'Let's get this sweater off.'

'O.K.,' said Allerton. He took off the sweater and then lay down again. Lee took off his own shoes and shirt. He opened Allerton's shirt and ran his hand down Allerton's ribs and stomach, which contracted beneath his fingers. 'God, you're skinny,' he said.

'I'm pretty small.'

Lee took off Allerton's shoes and socks. He loosened Allerton's belt and unbuttoned his trousers. Allerton arched his body, and Lee pulled the trousers and drawers off. He dropped his own trousers and shorts and lay down beside him. Allerton responded without hostility or disgust, but in his eyes Lee saw a curious detachment, the impersonal calm of an animal or a child.

Later, when they lay side by side smoking, Lee said, 'Oh, by the way, you said you had a camera in pawn you were about to lose?' It occurred to Lee that to bring the matter up at this time was not tactful, but he decided the other was not the type to take offense.

'Yes. In for four hundred pesos. The ticket runs out next Wednesday.'

'Well, let's go down tomorrow and get it out.'

Allerton raised one bare shoulder off the sheet. 'O.K.,' he said.

Chapter 4

Friday night Allerton went to work. He was taking his roommate's place proof reading for an English newspaper.

Saturday night Lee met Allerton in the Cuba, a bar with an interior like the set for a surrealist ballet. The walls were covered with murals depicting underwater scenes. Mermaids and mermen in elaborate arrangements with huge goldfish stared at the customers with fixed, identical expressions of pathic dismay. Even the fish were invested with an air of ineffectual alarm. The effect was disquieting, as though these androgynous beings were frightened by something behind or to one side of the customers, who were made uneasy by this inferred presence. Most of them took their business someplace else.

Allerton was somewhat sullen, and Lee felt depressed and ill at ease until he had put down two martinis. 'You know, Allerton ...,' he said after a long silence. Allerton was humming to himself, drumming on the table and looking around restlessly. Now he stopped humming, and raised an eyebrow.

'This punk is getting too smart,' Lee thought. He

knew he had no way of punishing him for indifference or insolence.

'They have the most incompetent tailors in Mexico I have encountered in all my experience as a traveller. Have you had any work done?' Lee looked pointedly at Allerton's shabby clothes. He was as careless of his clothes as Lee was. 'Apparently not. Take this tailor I'm hung up with. Simple job. I bought a pair of ready-made trousers. Never took time for a fitting. Both of us could get in those pants.'

'It wouldn't look right.' said Allerton.

'People would think we were Siamese twins. Did I ever tell you about the Siamese twin who turned his brother in to the law to get him off the junk? But to get back to this tailor. I took the pants in with another pair. "These pants is too voluminous," I told him. "I want them sewed down to the same size as this other pair here." He promised to do the job in two days. That was more than two months ago. '*Mañana*', '*más tarde*', '*ahora*', '*ahorita*', and every time I come to pick up the pants it's '*todavía no*' – not yet. Yesterday I had all the '*ahora*' routine I can stand still for. So I told him, "Ready or no, give me my pants." The pants was all cut down the seams. I told him, "Two months and all you have done is disembowel my trousers." I took them to another tailor and told him, "Sew them up." Are you hungry?'

'I am, as a matter of fact.'

'How about Pat's Steak House?'

'Good idea.'

Pat's served excellent steaks. Lee liked the place because it was never crowded. At Pat's he ordered a double dry martini. Allerton had rum and Coke. Lee began talking about telepathy.

'I know telepathy to be a fact, since I have experienced it myself. I have no interest to prove it, or, in fact, to prove anything to anybody. What interests me is, how can I use it? In South America at the headwaters of the Amazon grows a plant called Yage that is supposed to increase telepathic sensitivity. Medicine men use it in their work. A Colombian scientist, whose name escapes me, isolated from Yage a drug he called Telepathine. I read all this in a magazine article.

'Later I see another article – the Russians are using Yage in experiments on slave labor. It seems they want to induce states of automatic obedience and ultimately, of course, thought control. The basic con. No buildup, no spiel, no routine, just move in on someone's psyche and give orders. I have a theory the Mayan priests developed a form of one-way telepathy to con the peasants into doing all the work. The deal is certain to backfire eventually, because telepathy is not of its nature a one-way setup, nor a setup of sender and receiver at all.

'By now the U.S. is experimenting with Yage, unless they are dumber even than I think. Yage may be a means to usable knowledge of telepathy. Anything that can be accomplished chemically can be accomplished in other ways.' Lee saw that Allerton was not especially interested, and dropped the subject.

'Did you read about the old Jew who tried to smuggle out ten pounds of gold sewed in his overcoat?'

'No. What about it?'

'Well, this old Jew was nailed at the airport on his way to Cuba. I hear they got like a mine finder out at the airport rings a bell if anybody passes the gate with an outlandish quantity of metal on his person. So it says in the papers, after they give this Jew a shake and find the gold, a large number of Jewish-looking foreigners were seen looking into the airport window in a state of excitement. 'Oy, gefilte fish! They are putting the snatch on Abe!' Back in Roman times the Jews rose up – in Jerusalem I think it was – and killed fifty thousand Romans. The she-Jews – that is, the young Jewish ladies, I must be careful not to lay myself open to a charge of anti-Semitism – done strip teases with Roman intestines.

'Speaking of intestines, did I ever tell you about my friend Reggie? One of the unsung heroes of British Intelligence. Lost his ass and ten feet of lower intestine in the service. Lived for years disguised as an Arab boy known only as 'Number 69' at headquarters. That was wishful thinking, though, because the Arabs are strictly one way. Well, a rare Oriental disease set in, and poor Reggie lost the bulk of his tripes. For God and country, what? He didn't want any speeches, any medals, just to know that he had served, that was enough. Think of those patient years, waiting for another piece of the jigsaw puzzle to fall into place.

'You never hear of operators like Reggie, but it is their information, gathered in pain and danger, that gives some front-line general the plan for a brilliant counter-offensive and covers his chest with medals. For example, Reggie was the first to guess the enemy was running short of petrol when the K.Y. jelly gave out, and that was only one of his brilliant coups. How about the T-bone steak for two?'

'That's fine.'

'Rare?'

'Medium rare.'

Lee was looking at the menu. 'They list baked Alaska,' he said. 'Ever eat it?'

'No.'

'Real good. Hot on the outside and cold inside.'

'That's why they call it baked Alaska I imagine.'

'Got an idea for a new dish. Take a live pig and throw it into a very hot oven so the pig is roasted outside and when you cut into it, it's still alive and twitching inside. Or, if we run a dramatic joint, a screaming pig covered with burning brandy rushes out of the kitchen and dies right by your chair. You can reach down and pull off the crispy, crackly ears and eat them with your cocktails.'

Outside, the City lay under a violet haze. A warm spring wind blew through the trees in the park. They walked through the park back to Lee's place, occasionally stopping to lean against each other, weak from laughing. A Mexican said, '*Cabrones*,' as he walked by. Lee called after him, '*Chinga tu madre*,' then added in English. 'Here I come to your little jerkwater country and spend my good American dollars and what happens? Insulted inna public street.' The Mexican turned, hesitating, Lee unbuttoned his coat and hooked his thumb under the pistol at his waistband. The Mexican walked on.

'Someday they won't walk away,' said Lee.

At Lee's apartment they had some brandy. Lee put his arm around Allerton's shoulder.

'Well, if you insist,' said Allerton.

Sunday night Allerton had dinner at Lee's apartment. Lee cooked chicken livers, because Allerton always wanted to order chicken liver in restaurants, and usually restaurant chicken liver isn't fresh. After dinner Lee began making love to Allerton, but he rejected Lee's advances and said he wanted to go to the Ship Ahoy and drink a rum Coke. Lee turned out the light and embraced Allerton before they started out the door. Allerton's body was rigid with annoyance.

When they arrived at the Ship Ahoy, Lee went to the bar and ordered two rum Cokes. 'Make those extra strong,' he said to the bartender.

Allerton was sitting at a table with Mary. Lee brought the rum Coke over and set it down by Allerton. Then he sat down at a table with Joe Guidry. Joe Guidry had a young man with him. The young man was telling how he was treated by an Army psychiatrist. 'So what did you find out from your psychiatrist?' said Guidry. His voice had a nagging, derogatory edge.

'I found out I was an Oedipus. I found out I love my mother.'

'Why, everybody loves their mother, son,' said Guidry.

'I mean I love my mother physically,'

'I don't believe that, son,' said Guidry. This struck Lee as funny, and he began to laugh.

'I hear Jim Cochan has gone back to the States,' said Guidry. 'He plans to work in Alaska.'

'Thank God I am a gentleman of independent means, and don't have to expose myself to the inclemencies of near-Arctic conditions,' said Lee. 'By the way, did you ever meet Jim's wife, Alice? My god, she is an American bitch that won't quit. I never yet see her equal. Jim does not have one friend he can take to the house. She has forbidden him to eat out, as she does not want he should take in any nourishment unless she is there to watch him eat it. Did you ever hear the likes of that? Needless to say, my place is out of bounds to Jim, and he always has that hunted look when he comes to see me. I don't know why American men put up with such shit from a woman. Of course I am no expert judge of female flesh, but Alice has "lousy lay" written all over her scrawny, unappetizing person.'

'You're coming on mighty bitchy tonight, Lee,' said Guidry.

'And not without reason. Did I tell you about this Wigg person? He is an American hipster around town, a junky who is said to play a cool bass fiddle. Strictly on the chisel, even though he has gold, and he's always mooching junk, saying "No, I don't want to *buy* any. I'm kicking. I just want half a fix." I have had all I can stand still for from this character. Driving around in a new three-thousand-dollar Chrysler, and too cheap to buy his own junk. What am I, the Junky's Benevolent Society for christ sake? This Wigg is as ugly as people get.'

'You making it with him?' asked Guidry, which seemed to shock his young friend.

'Not even. I got bigger fish to fry,' said Lee. He glanced over at Allerton, who was laughing at something Mary had said.

'Fish is right,' quipped Guidry. 'Cold, slippery, and hard to catch.'

Chapter 5

Lee had an appointment with Allerton for eleven o'clock Monday morning to go the National Pawn Shop and get his camera out of hock. Lee came to Allerton's room and woke him up exactly at eleven. Allerton was sullen. He seemed on the point of going back to sleep. Finally Lee said, 'Well, are you going to get up now, or . . .'

Allerton opened his eyes and blinked like a turtle. 'I'm getting up,' he said.

Lee sat down and read a newspaper, careful to avoid watching Allerton dress. He was trying to control his hurt and anger, and the effort exhausted him. A heavy drag slowed movement and thought. Lee's face was rigid, his voice toneless. The strain continued through breakfast. Allerton sipped tomato juice in silence.

It took all day to get the camera. Allerton had lost the ticket. They went from one office to another. The officials shook their heads and drummed on the table, waiting. Lee put out two hundred pesos extra in bites. He finally paid the four hundred pesos, plus interest and various charges. He handed the camera to Allerton, who took it without comment.

They went back to the Ship Ahoy in silence. Lee went in and ordered a drink. Allerton disappeared. About an hour later he came in and sat with Lee.

'How about dinner tonight?' asked Lee.

Allerton said, 'No, I think I'll work tonight.'

Lee was depressed and shattered. The warmth and laughter of Saturday night was lost, and he did not know why. In any relation of love or friendship Lee attempted to establish contact on the non-verbal level of intuition, a silent exchange of thought and feeling. Now Allerton had abruptly shut off contact, and Lee felt a physical pain as though a part of himself tentatively stretched out towards the other had been severed, and he was looking at the bleeding stump in shock and disbelief.

Lee said, 'Like the Wallace administration, I subsidize non-production. I will pay you twenty pesos not to work tonight.' Lee was able to develop the idea, but Allerton's impatient coolness stopped him. He fell silent, looking at Allerton with shocked, hurt eyes.

Allerton was nervous and irritable, drumming on the table and looking around. He did not himself understand why Lee annoyed him.

'How about a drink?' Lee said.

'No. Not now. Anyway, I have to go.'

Lee got up jerkily. 'Well, I'll see you,' he said. 'I'll see you tomorrow.'

'Yes. Good night.'

He left Lee standing there, trying to formulate a plan to keep Allerton from going, to make an appointment for the next day, to mitigate in some way the hurt he had received.

Allerton was gone. Lee felt for the back of his chair

and lowered himself into it, like a man weak from illness. He stared at the table, his thoughts slow, as if he were very cold.

The bartender placed a sandwich in front of Lee. 'Huh?' said Lee. 'What's this?'

'The sandwich you ordered.'

'Oh, yes.' Lee took a few bites out of the sandwich, washing it down with water. 'On my bill, Joe,' he called to the bartender.

He got up and walked out. He walked slowly. Several times he leaned on a tree, looking at the ground as if his stomach hurt. Inside his apartment he took off his coat and shoes, and sat down on the bed. His throat began to ache, moisture hit his eyes, and he fell across the bed, sobbing convulsively. He pulled his knees up and covered his face with his hands, the fists clenched. Towards morning he turned on his back and stretched out. The sobs stopped, and his face relaxed in the morning light.

Lee woke up around noon, and sat for a long time on the edge of the bed with one shoe dangling from his hand. He dabbed water on his eyes, put on his coat, and went out.

Lee went down to the Zócalo and wandered around for several hours. His mouth was dry. He went into a Chinese restaurant, sat down in a booth and ordered a Coke. Misery spread through his body, now that he was sitting down with no motion to distract him. 'What happened?' he wondered.

He forced himself to look at the facts. Allerton was not queer enough to make a reciprocal relation possible. Lee's affection irritated him. Like many people who have nothing to do, he was resentful of any claims on his time. He had no close friends. He disliked definite appointments. He did not like to feel that anybody expected anything from him. He wanted, so far as possible, to live without external pressure. Allerton resented Lee's action in paying to recover the camera. He felt he was 'being sucked in on a phony deal,' and that an obligation he did not want had been thrust upon him.

Allerton did not recognize friends who made six-hundred-peso gifts, nor could he feel comfortable exploiting Lee. He made no attempt to clarify the situation. He did not want to see the contradiction involved in resenting a favor which he accepted. Lee found that he could tune in on Allerton's viewpoint, though the process caused him pain, since it involved seeing the extent of Allerton's indifference. 'I liked him and I wanted him to like me,' Lee thought. 'I wasn't trying to buy anything.'

'I have to leave town,' he decided. 'Go somewhere. Panama, South America.' He went down to the station to find out when the next train left for Veracruz. There was a train that night, but he did not buy a ticket. A feeling of cold desolation came over him at the thought of arriving alone in another country, far away from Allerton.

Lee took a cab to the Ship Ahoy. Allerton was not there, and Lee sat at the bar for three hours, drinking. Finally Allerton looked in the door, waved to Lee vaguely, and went upstairs with Mary. Lee knew they had probably gone to the owner's apartment, where they often ate dinner.

He went up to Tom Weston's apartment. Mary and Allerton were there. Lee sat down and tried to engage Allerton's interest, but he was too drunk to make sense. His attempt to carry on a casual, humorous conversation was painful to watch.

He must have slept. Mary and Allerton were gone. Tom Weston brought him some hot coffee. He drank the coffee, got up and staggered out of the apartment. Exhausted, he slept till the following morning.

Scenes from the chaotic, drunken month passed before his eyes. There was a face he did not recognize, a good-looking kid with amber eyes, yellow hair and beautiful straight black eyebrows. He saw himself asking someone he barely knew to buy him a beer in a bar on Insurgentes, and getting a nasty brush. He saw himself pull a gun on someone who followed him out of a clip joint on Coahuila and tried to roll him. He felt the friendly, steadying hands of people who had helped him home. 'Take it easy, Bill.' His childhood friend Rollins standing there, solid and virile, with his elkhound. Carl running for a streetcar. Moor with his malicious bitch smile. The faces blended together in a nightmare, speaking to him in strange moaning idiot voices that he could not understand at first, and finally could not hear.

Lee got up and shaved and felt better. He found he could eat a roll and drink some coffee. He smoked and read the paper, trying not to think about Allerton. Presently he went downtown and looked through the gun store. He found a bargain in a Colt Frontier, which he bought for two hundred pesos. A 32-20 in perfect condition, serial number in the three hundred thousands. Worth at least a hundred dollars Stateside.

Lee went to the American bookstore and bought a book on chess. He took the book out to Chapultepec, sat down in a soda stand on the lagoon, and began to read. Directly in front of him was an island with a huge cypress tree growing on it. Hundreds of vultures roosted in the tree. Lee wondered what they ate. He threw a piece of bread, which landed on the island. The vultures paid no attention.

Lee was interested in the theory of games and the strategy of random behavior. As he had supposed, the theory of games does not apply to chess, since chess rules out the element of chance and approaches elimination of the unpredictable human factor. If the mechanism of chess were completely understood, the outcome could be predicted after any initial move. 'A game for thinking machines,' Lee thought. He read on, smiling from time to time. Finally he got up, sailed the book out over the lagoon, and walked away.

Lee knew he could not find what he wanted with Allerton. The court of fact had rejected his petition. But Lee could not give up. 'Perhaps I can discover a way to change fact,' he thought. He was ready to take any risk, to proceed to any extreme of action. Like a saint or a wanted criminal with nothing to lose, Lee had stepped beyond the claims of his nagging, cautious, aging, frightened flesh.

He took a taxi to the Ship Ahoy. Allerton was standing in front of the Ship Ahoy, blinking sluggishly in the sunlight. Lee looked at him and smiled. Allerton smiled back.

'How are you?'

'Sleepy. Just got up.' He yawned and started into the Ship Ahoy. He moved one hand – 'See you' – and sat down at the bar and ordered tomato juice. Lee went in and sat beside him, and ordered a double rum Coke. Allerton moved and sat down at a table with Tom Weston. 'Bring the tomato juice over here, will you, Joe?' he called to the bartender.

Lee sat at the table next to Allerton's. Tom Weston was leaving. Allerton followed him out. He came back in and sat in the other room, reading the papers. Mary came in and sat down with him. After talking for a few minutes, they set up the chess board.

Lee had thrown down three drinks. He walked over and pulled up a chair to the table where Mary and Allerton were playing chess. 'Howdy,' he said. 'Don't mind if I kibitz?'

Mary looked up annoyed, but smiled when she met Lee's steady, reckless gaze.

'I was reading up on chess. Arabs invented it, and I'm not surprised. Nobody can sit like an Arab. The classical Arab chess game was simply a sitting contest. When both contestants starved to death it was a stalemate.' Lee paused and took a long drink.

'During the Baroque period of chess the practice of harrying your opponent with some annoying mannerism came into general use. Some players used dental floss, others cracked their joints or blew saliva bubbles. The method was constantly developed. In the 1917 match at Baghdad, the Arab Arachnid Khayam defeated the German master Kurt Schlemiel by humming "I'll Be Around When You're Gone" forty-thousand times, and each time reaching his hand towards the board as if he intended to make a move. Schlemiel went into convulsions finally.

'Did you ever have the good fortune to see the Italian master Tetrazzini perform?' Lee lit Mary's cigarette. 'I say "perform" advisedly, because he was a great showman, and like all showmen, not above

charlatanism and at times downright trickery. Sometimes he used smoke screens to hide his maneuvers
from the opposition – I mean literal smoke screens, of
course. He had a corps of trained idiots who would
rush in at a given signal and eat all the pieces. With
defeat staring him in the face – as it often did, because
actually he knew nothing of chess but the rules and
wasn't too sure of those – he would leap up yelling,
"You cheap bastard! I saw you palm that queen!" and
ram a broken teacup into his opponent's face. In 1922
he was rid out of Prague on a rail. The next time I saw
Tetrazzini was in the Upper Ubangi. A complete
wreck. Peddling unlicensed condoms. That was the
year of the rinderpest, when everything died, even the
hyenas.'

Lee paused. The routine was coming to him like
dictation. He did not know what he was going to say
next, but he suspected the monologue was about to get
dirty. He looked at Mary. She was exchanging signifi-
cant glances with Allerton. 'Some sort of lover code,'
Lee decided. 'She is telling him they have to go now.'
Allerton got up, saying he had to have a haircut before
going to work. Mary and Allerton left. Lee was alone in
the bar.

The monologue continued. 'I was working as Aide-
de-camp under General Von Klutch. Exacting. A hard
man to satisfy. I gave up trying after the first week. We
had a saying around the wardroom: "Never expose
your flank to old Klutchy." Well, I couldn't take Klutchy another night, so I assembled a modest caravan
and hit the trail with Abdul, the local Adonis. Ten
miles out of Tanhajaro, Abdul came down with the
rinderpest and I had to leave him there to die. Hated
to do it, but there was no other way. Lost his looks
competely, you understand.

'At the headwaters of the Zambesi, I ran into an old Dutch trader. After considerable haggling I gave him a keg of paregoric for a boy, half Effendi and half Lulu. I figured the boy would get me as far as Timbuktu, maybe all the way to Dakar. But the Lulu-Effendi was showing signs of wear even before I hit Timbuktu, and I decided to trade him in on a straight Bedouin model. The crossbreeds make a good appearance, but they don't hold up. In Timbuktu I went to Corn Hole Gus's Used-Slave Lot to see what he could do for me on a trade-in.

'Gus rushes out and goes into the spiel: "Ah, Sahib Lee. Allah has sent you! I have something right up your ass, I mean, alley. Just came in. One owner and he was a doctor. A once-over-lightly, twice-a-week-type citizen. It's young and it's tender. In fact, it talks baby talk . . . behold!"

'"You call those senile slobberings baby talk? My grandfather got a clap off that one. Come again, Gussie."

'"You do not like it? A pity. Well, everyone has a taste, feller say. Now here I have a one-hundred-percent desert-bred Bedouin with a pedigree goes straight back to the Prophet. Dig his bearing. Such pride! Such fire!"

'"A good appearance job, Gus, but not good enough. It's an albino Mongolian idiot. Look, Gussie, you are dealing with the oldest faggot in the Upper Ubangi, so come off the peg. Reach down into your grease pit and dredge out the best-looking punk you got in this moth-eaten bazaar."

'"All right Sahib Lee, you want quality, right? Follow me, please. Here it is. What can I say? Quality speaks for itself. Now, I get a lotta cheap-type customers in here wanna see quality and then scream at the price.

But you know and I know that quality runs high. As a matter of fact, and this I swear by the Prophet's prick, I lose money on this quality merchandise."

'"Uh huh. Got some hidden miles on him, but he'll do. How about a trial run?"

'"Lee, for christ sake, I don't run a house. This joint is strictly package. No consumption on premises. I could lose my license."

'"I don't aim to get caught short with one of your Scotch-tape and household-cement reconditioned jobs a hundred miles from the nearest Soukh. Besides, how do I know it ain't a Liz?"

'"Sahib Lee! This is an ethical lot!"

'"I was beat that way one time in Marrakesh. Citizen passed a transvestite Jew Lizzie on me as an Abyssinian prince."

'"Ha ha ha, full of funny jokes, aren't you? How is this: stay over in town tonight and try it out. If you don't want it in the morning, I refund every piaster. Fair enough?"

'"O.K., now, what can you give me on this Lulu-Effendi? Perfect condition. Just overhauled. He don't eat much and he don't say nothing."

'"Jesus, Lee! You know I'd cut off my right nut for you, but I swear by my mother's cunt, may I fall down and be paralysed and my prick fall off if these mixed jobs ain't harder to move than a junky's bowels."

'"Skip the routine. How much?"

'Gus stands in front of the Lulu-Effendi with his hands on his hips. He smiles and shakes his head. He walks around the boy. He reaches in and points to a small, slightly varicose vein behind the knee. "Look at that," he says, still smiling and shaking his head. He walks around again . . . "Got piles too." He shakes his head. "I don't know. I really don't know what to say to you. Open up, kid ... Two teeth missing." Gus has stopped smiling. He is talking in low, considerate tones, like an undertaker.

'"I'm going to be honest with you, Lee. I've got a lotful of this stuff now. I'd rather just forget this job and talk cash on the other."

'"What am I going to with it? Peddle it on the public street?"

'"Might take it along as a spare. Ha, ha ..."

'"Ha. What can you give me?"

'"Well ... now don't get mad ... two hundred piasters." Gus makes a skittish little run as if to escape my anger, and throws up a huge cloud of dust in the courtyard.'

The routine ended suddenly, and Lee looked around. The bar was nearly empty. He paid for his drinks and walked out into the night.

Chapter 6

Thursday Lee went to the races, on the recommendation of Tom Weston. Weston was an amateur astrologer, and he assured Lee the signs were right. Lee lost five races, and took a taxi back to the Ship Ahoy.

Mary and Allerton were sitting at a table with the Peruvian chess player. Allerton asked Lee to come over and sit down at the table.

'Where's that phony whore caster?' Lee said, looking around.

'Tom give you a bum steer?' asked Allerton.

'He did that.'

Mary left with the Peruvian. Lee finished his third drink and turned to Allerton. 'I figure to go down to South America soon,' he said. 'Why don't you come along? Won't cost you a cent.'

'Perhaps not in money.'

'I'm not a difficult man to get along with. We could reach a satisfactory arrangement. What you got to lose?'

'Independence.'

'So who's going to cut in on your independence? You can lay all the women in South America if you want to. All I ask is be nice to Papa, say twice a week.

That isn't excessive, is it? Besides, I will buy you a round-trip ticket so you can leave at your discretion.'

Allerton shrugged. 'I'll think it over,' he said. 'This job runs ten days more. I'll give you a definite answer when the job folds.'

'Your job . . .' Lee was about to say, 'I'll give you ten days' salary.' He said, 'All right.'

Allerton's newspaper job was temporary, and he was too lazy to hold a job in any case. Consequently his answer meant 'No.' Lee figured to talk him over in ten days. 'Better not force the issue now,' he thought.

Allerton planned a three-day trip to Morelia with his co-workers in the newspaper office. The night before he left, Lee was in a state of manic excitement. He collected a noisy table full of people. Allerton was playing chess with Mary, and Lee made all the noise he could. He kept his table laughing, but they all looked vaguely uneasy, as if they would prefer to be someplace else. They thought Lee was a little crazy. But just when he seemed on the point of some scandalous excess of speech or behavior, he would check himself and say something completely banal.

Lee leaped up to embrace a new arrival. 'Ricardo! *Amigo mío!*' he said. 'Haven't seen you in a dog's age. Where you been? Having a baby? Sit down on your ass, or what's left of it after four years in the Navy. What's troubling you, Richard? Is it women? I'm glad you came to me instead of those quacks on the top floor.'

At this point Allerton and Mary left, after consulting for a moment in low tones. Lee looked after them in silence. 'I'm playing to an empty house now,' he thought. He ordered another rum and swallowed four

Benzedrine tablets. Then he went into the head and smoked a roach of tea. 'Now I will ravish my public,' he thought.

The busboy had caught a mouse and was holding it up by the tail. Lee pulled out an old-fashioned .22 revolver he sometimes carried. 'Hold the son of a bitch out and I'll blast it,' he said, striking a Napoleonic pose. The boy tied a string to the mouse's tail and held it out at arm's length. Lee fired from a distance of three feet. His bullet tore the mouse's head off.

'If you'd got any closer the mouse would have clogged the muzzle,' said Richard.

Tom Weston came in. 'Here comes the old whore caster,' Lee said. 'That retrograde Saturn dragging your ass, man?'

'My ass is dragging because I need a beer,' said Weston.

'Well, you've come to the right place. A beer for my astrologizing friend ... What's that? I'm sorry, old man,' Lee said, turning to Weston, 'but the bartender say the signs aren't right to serve you a beer. You see, Venus is in the sixty-ninth house with a randy Neptune and he couldn't let you have a beer under such auspices.' Lee washed down a small piece of opium with black coffee.

Horace walked in and gave Lee his brief, cold nod. Lee rushed over and embraced him. 'This thing is bigger than both of us, Horace,' he said. 'Why hide our love?'

Horace thrust out his arms rigidly. 'Knock it off,' he said. 'Knock it off.'

'Just a Mexican *abrazo*, Horace. Custom to the country. Everyone does it down here.'

'I don't care what the custom is. Just keep away from me.'

'Horace! Why are you so cold?'

Horace said, 'Knock it off, will you?' and walked out. A little later he came back and stood at the end of the bar drinking a beer.

Weston and Al and Richard came over and stood with Lee. 'We're with you, Bill,' Weston said. 'If he lays a finger on you I'll break a beer bottle over his head.'

Lee did not want to push the routine past a joking stage. He said, 'Oh, Horace is okay, I guess. But there's a limit to what I can stand still for. Two years he hands me these curt nods. Two years he walks into Lola's and looks around – "Nothing in here but fags," he says and goes out on the street to drink his beer. Like I say, there is a limit.'

Allerton came back from his trip to Morelia sullen and irritable. When Lee asked if he had a good trip, he muttered, 'Oh, all right,' and went in the other room to play chess with Mary. Lee felt a charge of anger pass through his body. 'I'll make him pay for this somehow,' he thought.

Lee considered buying a half-interest in the Ship Ahoy. Allerton existed on credit at the Ship Ahoy, and owed four hundred pesos. If Lee was half-owner of the joint, Allerton would not be in a position to ignore him. Lee did not actually want retaliation. He felt a desperate need to maintain some special contact with Allerton.

Lee managed to re-establish contact. One afternoon Lee and Allerton went to visit Al Hyman, who was in the hospital with jaundice. On the way home they stopped in the Bottoms Up for a cocktail.

'What about this trip to South America?' Lee said abruptly.

'Well, it's nice to see places you haven't seen before,' said Allerton.

'Can you leave anytime?'

'Anytime.'

Next day Lee started collecting the necessary visas and tickets. 'Better buy some camping equipment here,' he said. 'We may have to trek back into the jungle to find the Yage. When we get where the Yage is, we'll dig a hip cat and ask him, "Where can we score for Yage?"'

'How will you know where to look for the Yage?'

'I aim to find that out in Bogotá. A Colombian scientist who lives in Bogotá isolated Telepathine from Yage. We must find that scientist.'

'Suppose he won't talk?'

'They all talk when Boris goes to work on them.'

'You Boris?'

'Certainly not. We pick up Boris in Panama. He did excellent work with the Reds in Barcelona and with the Gestapo in Poland. A talented man. All his work has the Boris touch. Light, but persuasive. A mild little fellow with spectacles. Looks like a book-keeper. I met him in a Turkish bath in Budapest.'

A blond Mexican boy went by pushing a cart. 'Jesus Christ!' Lee said, his mouth dropping open. 'One of them blond-headed Mexicans! 'Tain't as if it was being queer, Allerton. After all, they's only Mexicans. Let's have a drink.'

*

They left by bus a few days later, and by the time they reached Panama City, Allerton was already complaining that Lee was too demanding in his desires. Otherwise, they got on very well. Now that Lee could spend days and nights with the object of his attentions, he felt relieved of the gnawing emptiness and fear. And Allerton was a good travelling companion, sensible and calm.

Chapter 7

They flew from Panama to Quito, in a tiny plane which had to struggle to climb above an overcast. The steward plugged in the oxygen. Lee sniffed the oxygen hose. 'It's cut!' he said in disgust.

They drove into Quito in a windy, cold twilight. The hotel looked a hundred years old. The room had a high ceiling with black beams and white plaster walls. They sat on the beds, shivering. Lee was a little junk sick.

They walked around the main square. Lee hit a drugstore – no paregoric without a script. A cold wind from the high mountains blew rubbish through the dirty streets. The people walked by in gloomy silence. Many had blankets wrapped around their faces. A row of hideous old hags, huddled in dirty blankets that looked like old burlap sacks, were ranged along the walls of a church.

'Now, son, I want you to know I am different from other citizens you might run into. Some people will give you the women-are-no-good routine. I'm not like that. You just pick yourself one of these *señoritas* and take her right back to the hotel with you.'

Allerton looked at him. 'I think I will get laid tonight,' he said.

'Sure,' Lee said. 'Go right ahead. They don't have much pulchritude in this dump, but that hadn't oughta deter you young fellers. Was it Frank Harris said he never saw an ugly woman till he was thirty? It was, as a matter of fact . . . Let's go back to the hotel and have a drink.'

The bar was drafty. Oak chairs with black leather seats. They ordered martinis. At the next table a red-faced American in an expensive brown gabardine suit was talking about some deal involving twenty thousand acres. Across from Lee was an Ecuadoran man, with a long nose and a spot of red on each cheekbone, dressed in a black suit of European cut. He was drinking coffee and eating sweet cakes.

Lee drank several cocktails. He was getting sicker by the minute. 'Why don't you smoke some weed?' Allerton suggested. 'That might help.'

'Good idea. Let's go up to the room.'

Lee smoked a stick of tea on the balcony. 'My god, is it cold out on that balcony,' he said, coming back into the room.

'". . . And when twilight falls on the beautiful old colonial city of Quito and those cool breezes steal down from the Andes, walk out in the fresh of the evening and look over the beautiful *señoritas* who seat themselves, in colorful native costume, along the wall of the sixteenth-century church that overlooks the main square . . .' They fired the guy wrote that. There *are* limits, even in a travel folder . . .

'Tibet must be about like this. High and cold and full of ugly-looking people and llamas and yaks. Yak milk for breakfast, yak curds for lunch, and for dinner a yak boiled in his own butter, and a fitting punishment for a yak, too, if you ask me.

'You can smell one of those holy men ten miles downwind on a clear day. Sitting there pulling on his old prayer wheel so nasty. Wrapped in dirty old burlap sacks, with bedbugs crawling around where his neck sticks out of the sack. His nose is all rotted away and he spits betel nut out through the nose holes like a spitting cobra . . . Give me that Wisdom-of-the-East routine.

'So we got like a holy man and some bitch reporter comes to interview him. He sits there chewing on his betel nut. After a while, he says to one of his acolytes, "Go down to the Sacred Well and bring me a dipper of paregoric. I'm going to make with the Wisdom of the East. And shake the lead out of your loin cloth!" So he drinks the P.G. and goes into a light trance, and makes cosmic contact – we call it going on the nod in the trade. The reporter says, "Will there be war with Russia, Mahatma? Will Communism destroy the civilized world? Is the soul immortal? Does God exist?"

'The Mahatma opens his eyes and compresses his lips and spits two long, red streams of betel nut juice out through his nose holes. It runs down over his mouth and he licks it back in with a long, coated tongue and says, "How in the fuck should I know?" The acolyte says, "You heard the man. Now cut. The Swami wants to be alone with his medications." Come to think of it, that *is* the wisdom of the East. The Westerner thinks there is some secret he can discover. The East says, "How the fuck should I know?"'

That night Lee dreamed he was in a penal colony. All around were high, bare mountains. He lived in a boardinghouse that was never warm. He went out for a walk. As he stepped off a streetcorner onto a dirty cobblestone street, the cold mountain wind hit him. He tightened the belt of his leather jacket and felt the chill of final despair.

Lee woke up and called to Allerton, 'Are you awake, Gene?'

'Yes.'

'Cold?'

'Yes.'

'Can I come over with you?'

'Ahh, well all right.'

Lee got in bed with Allerton. He was shaking with cold and junk sickness.

'You're twitching all over,' said Allerton. Lee pressed against him, convulsed by the adolescent lust of junk sickness.

'Christ almighty, your hands are cold.'

When Allerton was asleep, he rolled over and threw his knee across Lee's body. Lee lay still so he wouldn't wake up and move away.

The next day Lee was really sick. They wandered around Quito. The more Lee saw of Quito, the more the place brought him down. The town was hilly, the streets narrow. Allerton stepped off the high curb and a car grazed him. 'Thank god you're not hurt,' Lee said. 'I sure would hate to be stuck in this town.'

They sat down in a little coffeehouse where some German refugees hung out, talking about visas and extensions and work permits, and got into a conversation with a man at the next table. The man was thin and blond, his head caved in at the temples. Lee could see the blue veins pulsing in the cold, high-mountain sunlight that covered the man's weak, ravaged face and spilled over the scarred oak table onto the worn wooden floor. Lee asked the man if he liked Quito.

'To be or not to be, that is the question. I have to like it.'

They walked out of the coffeehouse, and up the street to a park. The trees were stunted by wind and cold. A few boys were rowing around and around in a small pond. Lee watched them, torn by lust and curiosity. He saw himself desperately rummaging through bodies and rooms and closets in a frenzied search, a recurrent nightmare. At the end of the search was an empty room. He shivered in the cold wind.

Allerton said, 'Why don't you ask in the coffee shop for the name of a doctor?'

'That's a good idea.'

The doctor lived in a yellow stucco villa on a quiet side street. He was Jewish, with a smooth, red face, and spoke good English. Lee put down a dysentery routine. The doctor asked a few questions. He started to write out a prescription. Lee said, 'The prescription that works best is paregoric with bismuth.'

The doctor laughed. He gave Lee a long look. Finally he said, 'Tell the truth now.' He raised a forefinger, smiling. 'Are you addicted to opiates? Better you tell me. Otherwise I cannot help you.'

Lee said, 'Yes.'

'Ah ha,' said the doctor, and he crumpled up the prescription he was writing and dropped it in the wastebasket. He asked Lee how long the addiction had lasted. He shook his head, looking at Lee.

'*Ach*,' he said, 'you are a young person. You must stop this habit. So you lose your life. Better you should suffer now than continue this habit.' The doctor gave Lee a long, human look.

'My god,' Lee thought, 'what you have to put up with in this business.' He nodded and said, 'Of course, Doctor, and I want to stop. But I have to get some sleep. I am going to the coast tomorrow, to Manta.'

The doctor sat back in his chair, smiling. 'You must stop this habit.' He ran through the routine again. Lee nodded abstractedly. Finally the doctor reached for his prescription pad: three c.c.'s of tincture.

The drugstore gave Lee paregoric instead of tincture. Three c.c.'s of P.G. Less than a teaspoonful. Nothing. Lee bought a bottle of antihistamine tablets and took a handful. They seemed to help a little.

Lee and Allerton took a plane the next day for Manta.

The Hotel Continental in Manta was made of split bamboo and rough boards. Lee found some knot-holes in the wall of their room, and plugged the holes up with paper. 'We don't want to get deported under a cloud,' he said to Allerton. 'I'm a little junk sick, you know, and that makes me sooo sexy. The neighbors could witness some innaresting sights.'

'I wish to register a complaint concerning breach of contract,' said Allerton. 'You said twice a week.'

'So I did. Well, of course the contract is more or less elastic you might say. But you are right. Twice a week it is, sire. Of course, if you get hot pants between times, don't hesitate to let me know.'

'I'll give you a buzz.'

The water was just right for Lee, who could not stand cold water. There was no shock when he plunged in. They swam for an hour or so, then sat on the beach looking at the sea. Allerton could sit for hours doing absolutely nothing. He said, 'That boat out there has been warming up for the past hour.'

'I am going into town to dig the local *bodegas* and buy a bottle of cognac,' Lee told him.

The town looked old, with limestone streets and dirty saloons crowded with sailors and dockworkers. A shoeshine boy asked Lee if he wanted a 'nice girl'. Lee looked at the boy and said in English, 'No, and I don't want you either.'

He bought a bottle of cognac from a Turkish trader. The store had everything: ship stores, hardware, guns, food, liquor. Lee priced the guns: three hundred dollars for a 30-30 lever-action Winchester carbine that sold for seventy-two dollars in the States. The Turk said duty was high on guns. That was the reason for this price.

Lee walked back along the beach. The houses were all split bamboo on wood frame, the four posts set directly in the ground. The simplest type of house construction: you set four heavy posts deep in the ground and nail the house to the posts. The houses were built about six feet off the ground. The streets were mud. Thousands of vultures roosted on the houses and walked around the streets, pecking at offal. Lee kicked at a vulture, and the bird flapped away with an indignant squawk.

Lee passed a bar, a large building built directly on the ground, and decided to go in for a drink. The split-bamboo walls shook with noise. Two middle-aged wiry little men were doing an obscene mambo routine opposite each other, their leathery faces creased in toothless smiles. The waiter came up and smiled at Lee. He didn't have any front teeth either. Lee sat down on a short wood bench and ordered a cognac.

A boy of sixteen or so came over and sat down with Lee and smiled an open, friendly smile. Lee smiled back and ordered a *refresco* for the boy. He dropped a hand on Lee's thigh and squeezed it in thanks for the drink. The boy had uneven teeth, crowded one over the other, but he was a young boy. Lee looked at him speculatively; he couldn't figure the score. Was the boy giving him a come-on, or was he just friendly? He knew that people in the Latin American countries were not self-conscious about physical contact. Boys walked around with their arms around each other's necks. Lee decided to play it cool. He finished his drink, shook hands with the boy, and walked back to the hotel.

Allerton was still sitting on the porch in his swimming trunks and a short-sleeved yellow short, which flapped around his thin body in the evening wind. Lee went inside to the kitchen and ordered ice and water and glasses. He told Allerton about the Turk, the town and the boy. 'Let's go dig that bar after dinner,' he said.

'And get felt up by those young boys?' said Allerton. 'I should say not.'

Lee laughed. He was feeling surprisingly well. The antihistamine cut his junk sickness to a vague malaise, something he would not have noticed if he did not know what it was. He looked out over the bay, red in the setting sun. Boats of all sizes were anchored in the bay. Lee wanted to buy a boat and sail up and down the coast. Allerton liked the idea.

'While we are in Ecuador we must score for Yage,' Lee said. 'Think of it: thought control. Take anyone apart and rebuild to your taste. Anything about somebody bugs you, you say, "Yage! I want that routine took clear out of his mind." I could think of a few changes I might make in you, doll.' He looked at Allerton and licked his lips. 'You'd be so much *nicer* after a few alterations. You're nice now, of course, but you do have those irritating little peculiarities. I mean, you won't do exactly what I want you to do all the time.'

'Do you think there is anything in it, really?' Allerton asked.

'The Russians seem to think so. I understand Yage is the efficient confession drug. They have also used peyote. Ever try it?'

'No.'

'Horrible stuff. Made me sick like I wanted to die. I got to puke and I can't. Just excruciating spasms of the asparagras, or whatever you call that gadget. Finally the peyote comes up solid like a ball of hair, solid all the way up, clogging my throat. As nasty a sensation as I ever stood still for. The high is interesting, but hardly worth the sick stage. Your face swells around the eyes, and the lips swell, and you look and feel like an Indian, or what you figure an Indian feels like. Primitive, you understand. Colors are more intense, but somehow flat and two-dimensional. Everything looks like a peyote plant. There is a nightmare undercurrent.

'I had nightmares after using it, one after the other, every time I went back to sleep. In one dream I had rabies and looked in the mirror and my face changed and I began howling. Another dream I had a chloro-phyll habit. Me and five other chlorophyll addicts are waiting to score. We turn green and we can't kick the chlorophyll habit. One shot and you are hung for life. We are turning into plants. You know anything about psychiatry? Schizophrenia?'

'Not much.'

'In some cases of schizophrenia a phenomenon occurs known as automatic obedience. I say, "Stick out your tongue," and you can't keep yourself from obeying. Whatever I say, whatever anyone says, you must do. Get the picture? A pretty picture, isn't it, so long as you are the one giving the orders that are automatically obeyed. Automatic obedience, synthetic schizophrenia, mass-produced to order. That is the Russian dream, and America is not far behind. The bureaucrats of both countries want the same thing: Control. The superego, the controlling agency, gone cancerous and berserk. Incidentally, there is a connection between schizophrenia and telepathy. Schizos are very telepathically sensitive, but are strictly *receivers*. Dig the tie-in?'

'But you wouldn't know Yage if you saw it?'

Lee thought a minute. 'Much as I dislike the idea. I will have to go back to Quito and talk to a botanist at the Botanical Institute there.'

'I'm not going back to Quito for anything,' said Allerton.

'I'm not going right away. I need some rest and I want to kick the Chinaman all the way out. No need for you to go. You stay on the beach. Papa will go and get the info.'

Chapter 8

From Manta they flew on to Guayaquil. The road was flooded, so the only way to get there was by plane or boat.

Guayaquil is built along a river, a city with many parks and squares and statues. The parks are full of tropical trees and shrubs and vines. A tree that fans out like an umbrella, as wide as it is tall, shades the stone benches. The people do a great deal of sitting.

One day Lee got up early and went to the market. The place was crowded. A curiously mixed populace: Negro, Chinese, Indian, European, Arab, characters difficult to classify. Lee saw some beautiful boys of mixed Chinese and Negro stock, slender and graceful with beautiful white teeth.

A hunchback with withered legs was playing crude bamboo panpipes, a mournful Oriental music with the sadness of the high mountains. In deep sadness there is no place for sentimentality. It is as final as the mountains: a fact. There it is. When you realize it, you cannot complain.

People crowded around the musician, listened a few minutes, and walked on. Lee noticed a young man with the skin tight over his small face, looking exactly like a shrunken head. He could not have weighed more than ninety pounds.

The musician coughed from time to time. Once he snarled when someone touched his hump, showing his black rotten teeth. Lee gave the man a few coins. He walked on, looking at every face he passed, looking into doorways and up at the windows of cheap hotels. An iron bedstead painted light pink, a shirt out to dry . . . scraps of life. Lee snapped at them hungrily, like a predatory fish cut off from his prey by a glass wall. He could not stop ramming his nose against the glass in the nightmare search of his dream. And at the end he was standing in a dusty room in the late afternoon sun, with an old shoe in his hand.

The city, like all Ecuador, produced a curiously baffling impression. Lee felt there was something going on here, some undercurrent of life that was hidden from him. This was the area of the ancient Chimu pottery, where salt shakers and water pitchers were nameless obscenities: two men on all fours engaged in sodomy formed the handle for the top of a kitchen pot.

What happens when there is no limit? What is the fate of The Land Where Anything Goes? Men changing into huge centipedes . . . centipedes besieging the houses . . . a man tied to a couch and a centipede ten feet long rearing up over him. Is this literal? Did some hideous metamorphosis occur? What is the meaning of the centipede symbol?

Lee got on a bus and rode to the end of the line. He took another bus. He rode out to the river and drank a soda, and watched some boys swimming in the dirty river. The river looked as if nameless monsters might rise from the green-brown water. Lee saw a lizard two feet long run up the opposite bank.

He walked back towards town. He passed a group of boys on a corner. One of the boys was so beautiful that the image cut Lee's senses like a wire whip. A slight involuntary sound of pain escaped from Lee's lips. He turned around, as though looking at the street name. The boy was laughing at some joke, a high-pitched laugh, happy and gay. Lee walked on.

Six or seven boys, aged twelve to fourteen, were playing in a heap of rubbish on the waterfront. One of the boys was urinating against a post and smiling at the other boys. The boys noticed Lee. Now their play was overtly sexual, with an undercurrent of mockery. They looked at Lee and whispered and laughed. Lee looked at them openly, a cold, hard stare of naked lust. He felt the tearing ache of limitless desire.

He focused on one boy, the image sharp and clear, as if seen through a telescope with the other boys and the waterfront blacked out. The boy vibrated with life like a young animal. A wide grin showed sharp, white teeth. Under the torn shirt Lee glimpsed the thin body.

He could feel himself in the body of the boy. Fragmentary memories . . . the smell of cocoa beans drying in the sun, bamboo tenements, the warm dirty river, the swamps and rubbish heaps on the outskirts of the town. He was with the other boys, sitting on the stone floor of a deserted house. The roof was gone. The stone walls were falling down. Weeds and vines grew over the walls and stretched across the floor.

The boys were taking down their torn pants. Lee lifted his thin buttocks to slip down his pants. He could feel the stone floor. He had his pants down to his ankles. His knees were clasped together, and the other boys were trying to pull them apart. He gave in, and they held his knees open. He looked at them and smiled, and slipped his hand down over his stomach. Another boy who was standing up dropped his pants and stood there with his hands on his hips, looking down at his erect organ.

A boy sat down by Lee and reached over between his legs. Lee felt the orgasm blackout in the hot sun. He stretched out and threw his arm over his eyes. Another boy rested his head on his stomach. Lee could feel the warmth of the other's head, itching a little where the hair touched Lee's stomach.

Now he was in a bamboo tenement. An oil lamp lit a woman's body. Lee could feel desire for the woman through the other's body. 'I'm not queer,' he thought. 'I'm disembodied.'

Lee walked on, thinking. 'What can I do? Take them back to my hotel? They are willing enough. For a few Sucres . . .' He felt a killing hate for the stupid, ordinary, disapproving people who kept him from doing what he wanted to do. 'Someday I am going to have things just like I want,' he said to himself. 'And if any moralizing son of a bitch gives me any static, they will fish him out of the river.'

Lee's plan involved a river. He lived on the river and ran things to please himself. He grew his own weed and poppies and cocaine, and he had a young native boy for an all-purpose servant. Boats were moored in the dirty river. Great masses of water hyacinths floated by. The river was a good half-mile across.

Lee walked up to a little park. There was a statue of Bolívar, 'The Liberating Fool' as Lee called him, shaking hands with someone else. Both of them looked tired and disgusted and rocking queer, so queer it rocked you. Lee stood looking at the statue. Then he sat down on a stone bench facing the river. Everyone looked at Lee when he sat down. Lee looked back. He did not have the American reluctance to meet the gaze of a stranger. The others looked away, and lit cigarettes and resumed their conversations.

Lee sat there looking at the dirty yellow river. He couldn't see half an inch under the surface. From time to time, small fish jumped ahead of a boat. There were trim, expensive sailing boats from the yacht club, with hollow masts and beautiful lines. There were dugout canoes with outboard motors and cabins of split bamboo. Two old rusty battleships were moored in the middle of the river – the Ecuadoran Navy. Lee sat there a full hour, then got up and walked back to the hotel. It was three o'clock. Allerton was still in bed. Lee sat down on the edge of the bed. 'It's three o'clock, Gene. Time to get up.'

'What for?'

'You want to spend your life in bed? Come on out and dig the town with me. I saw some beautiful boys on the waterfront. The real uncut stuff. Such teeth, such smiles. Young boys vibrating with life.'

'All right. Stop drooling.'

'What have they got that I want, Gene? Do you know?'

'No.'

'They have maleness, of course. So have I. I want myself the same way I want others. I'm disembodied. I can't use my own body for some reason.' He put out his hand. Allerton dodged away.

'What's the matter?'

'I thought you were going to run your hand down my ribs.'

'I wouldn't do that. Think I'm queer or something?'

'Frankly, yes.'

'You do have nice ribs. Show me the broken one. Is that it there?' Lee ran his hand halfway down

Allerton's ribs. 'Or is it further down?'

'Oh, go away.'

'But, Gene . . . I am due, you know.'

'Yes, I suppose you are.'

'Of course, if you'd rather wait until tonight. These tropical nights are so romantic. That way we could take twelve hours or so and do the thing right.' Lee ran his hands down over Allerton's stomach. He could see that Allerton was a little excited.

Allerton said, 'Maybe it would be better now. You know I like to sleep alone.'

'Yes, I know. Too bad. If I had my way we'd sleep every night all wrapped around each other like hibernating rattlesnakes.'

Lee was taking off his clothes. He lay down beside Allerton. 'Wouldn't it be booful if we should juth run together into one gweat big blob.' he said in baby talk. 'Am I giving you the horrors?'

'Indeed you are.'

Allerton surprised Lee by an unusual intensity of response. At the climax he squeezed Lee hard around the ribs. He sighed deeply and closed his eyes.

Lee smoothed his eyebrows with his thumbs. 'Do you mind that?' he asked.

'Not terribly.'

'But you do enjoy it sometimes? The whole deal, I mean.'

'Oh, yes.'

Lee lay on his back with one cheek against Allerton's shoulder, and went to sleep.

Lee decided to apply for a passport before leaving Guayaquil. He was changing clothes to visit the embassy, and talking to Allerton. 'Wouldn't do to wear high shoes. The Consul is probably an elegant pansy ... "My dear, can you believe it? High shoes. I mean real old button-hooky shoes. I simply couldn't take my eyes of those shoes. I'm afraid I have no idea what he wanted."

'I hear they are purging the State Department of queers. If they do, they will be operating with a skeleton staff ... ah, here they are.' Lee was putting on a pair of low shoes. 'Imagine walking in on the Consul and asking him right out for money to eat on ... He rears back and claps a scented handkerchief over his mouth, as if you had dropped a dead lobster on his desk: "You're broke! Really, I don't know why you come to me with this revolting disclosure. You might show a modicum of consideration. You must realize how distasteful this sort of thing is. Have you no pride?"'

Lee turned to Allerton. 'How do I look? Don't want to look too good, or he will be trying to get in my pants. Maybe *you*'d better go. That way we'll get our passports by tomorrow.'

'Listen to this.' Lee was reading from a Guayaquil paper. 'It seems that the Peruvian delegates at the anti-tuberculosis congress in Salinas appeared at the meeting carrying huge maps on which were shown the parts of Ecuador appropriated by Peru in the 1939 war. The Ecuadoran doctors might go to the meeting twirling shrunken heads of Peruvian soldiers on their watch chains.'

Allerton had found an article about the heroic fight put up by Ecuador's wolves of the sea.

'Their what?'

'That's what it says: *Lobos del Mar*. It seems that one officer stuck by his gun, even though the mechanism was no longer operating.'

'Sounds simpleminded to me.'

They decided to look for a boat in Las Playas. Las Playas was cold and the water was rough and muddy, a dreary middle-class resort. The food was terrible, but the room without meals was almost the same as full *pensión*. They tried one lunch. A plate of rice without sauce, without anything. Allerton said, 'I am hurt.' A tasteless soup with some fibrous material floating in it that looked like soft, white wood. The main course was a nameless meat as impossible to identify as to eat.

Lee said, 'The cook has barricaded himself in the kitchen. He is shoving this slop out through a slot.' The food was, as a matter of fact, passed out through a slot in a door from a dark, smoky room where, presumably, it was being prepared.

They decided they would go on to Salinas the next day. That night Lee wanted to go to bed with Allerton, but he refused and the next morning Lee said he was sorry he asked so soon after the last time, which was a breach of contract.

Allerton said, 'I don't like people who apologize at breakfast.'

Lee said, 'Really, Gene, aren't you taking an unfair advantage? Like someone was junk sick and I don't use junk. I say, "Sick, really? I don't know why you tell me about your disgusting condition. You might at least have the decency to keep it to yourself if you are sick. I hate sick people. You must realize how distasteful it is to see you sneezing and yawning and retching. Why don't you go someplace where I won't have to look at you? You've no idea how tiresome you are, or how disgusting. Have you no pride?"'

Allerton said, 'That isn't fair at all.'

'It isn't supposed to be fair. Just a routine for your amusement, containing a modicum of truth. Hurry and finish your breakfast. We'll miss the Salinas bus.'

Salinas had the quiet, dignified air of an upper-class resort town. They had come in the off season. When they went to swim they found out why this was not the season: the Humboldt current makes the water cold during the summer months. Allerton put his foot in the water and said, 'It's nothing but cold,' and refused to go in. Lee plunged in and swam for a few minutes.

Time seemed to speed up in Salinas. Lee would eat lunch and lie on the beach. After a period that seemed like an hour, or at most two hours, he saw the sun low in the sky: six o'clock. Allerton reported the same experience.

Lee went to Quito to get information on the Yage. Allerton stayed in Salinas. Lee was back five days later.

'Yage is also known to the Indians as Ayahuasca. Scientific name is *Bannisteria caapi*.' Lee spread a map out on the bed. 'It grows in high jungle on the Amazon side of the Andes. We will go on to Puyo. That is the end of the road. We should be able to locate someone there who can deal with the Indians, and get the Yage.'

They spent a night in Guayaquil. Lee got drunk before dinner and slept through a movie. They went back to the hotel to go to bed and get an early start in the morning. Lee poured himself some brandy and sat down on the edge of Allerton's bed. 'You look sweet tonight,' he said, taking off his glasses. How about a little kiss? Huh?'

'Oh, go away,' said Allerton.

'Okay kid, if you say so. There's plenty of time.' Lee poured some more brandy in his glass and lay down on his own bed.

'You know, Gene, not only have they got poor people in this jerkwater country. They also got like rich people. I saw some on the train going up to Quito. I expect they keep a plane revved up in the back yard. I can see them loading television sets and radios and golf clubs and tennis rackets and shotguns into the plane, and then trying to boot a prize Brahma bull in on top of the other junk, so the windup is the plane won't get off the ground.

'It's a small, unstable, undeveloped country. Economic setup exactly the way I figured it: all raw materials, lumber, food, labor, rent, very cheap. All manufactured goods very high, because of import duty. The duty is supposed to protect Ecuadoran industry. There is no Ecuadoran industry. No production here. The people who can produce won't produce because they don't want any money tied up here. They want to be ready to pull out right now, with a bundle of cold cash, preferably U.S. dollars. They are unduly alarmed. Rich people are generally frightened. I don't know why. Something to do with a guilt complex, I imagine. *¿Quién sabe?* I have not come to psychoanalyse Caesar, but to protect his person. At a price, of course. What they need here is a security department, to keep the underdog under.'

'Yes,' said Allerton. 'We must secure uniformity of opinion.'

'Opinion! What are we running here, a debating society? Give me one year and the people won't have any opinions. "Now just fall in line here folks, for your nice tasty stew of fish heads and rice and oleomargarine. And over here for your ration of free lush laced with opium." So if they get out of line, we jerk the junk out of the lush and they're all lying around shitting in their pants, too weak to move. An eating habit is the worst habit you can have. Another angle is malaria. A debilitating affliction, tailor-made to water down the revolutionary spirit.'

Lee smiled. 'Just imagine some old humanist German doctor. I say, "Well, Doc, you done a great job here with malaria. Cut the incidence down almost to nothing."

'"*Ach*, yes. We do our best, is it not? You see this line in the graph? The line shows the decline in this sickness in the past ten years since we commence with our treatment program."

'"Yeah, Doc. Now look, I want to see that line go back where it came from."

'"*Ach*, this you cannot mean."

'"And another thing. See if you can't import an especially debilitating strain of hookworm."

'The mountain people we can always immobilize by taking their blankets away, leaving them with the enterprise of a frozen lizard.'

The inside wall of Lee's room stopped about three feet from the ceiling to allow for ventilating the next room, which was an inside room with no windows. The occupant of the next room said something in Spanish to the effect Lee should be quiet.

'Ah, shut up,' said Lee, leaping to his feet. 'I'll nail a blanket over that slot! I'll cut off your fucking air! You only breathe with my permission. You're the occupant of an inside room, a room without windows. So remember your place and shut your poverty-stricken mouth!'

A stream of *chingas* and *cabrones* replied.

'*Hombre*,' Lee asked, '*¿En dónde está su cultura?*'

'Let's hit the sack,' said Allerton. 'I'm tired.'

Chapter 9

They took a river boat to Babahoya. Swinging in hammocks, sipping brandy, and watching the jungle slide by. Springs, moss, beautiful clear streams and trees up to two hundred feet high. Lee and Allerton were silent as the boat powered upriver, penetrating the jungle stillness with its lawnmower whine.

From Babahoya they took a bus over the Andes to Ambato, a cold, jolting fourteen-hour ride. They stopped for a snack of chick-peas at a hut at the top of the mountain pass, far above the tree line. A few young native men in gray felt hats ate their chick-peas in sullen resignation. Several guinea pigs were squeaking and scurrying around on the dirt floor of the hut. Their cries reminded Lee of the guinea pig he owned as a child in the Fairmont Hotel in St. Louis, when the family was waiting to move into their new house on Price Road. He remembered the way the pig shrieked, the stink of its cage.

They passed the snow-covered peak of Chimborazo, cold in the moonlight and the constant wind of the high Andes. The view from the high mountain pass seemed from another, larger planet than Earth. Lee and Allerton huddled together under a blanket, drinking brandy, the smell of wood smoke in their nostrils. They were both wearing Army-surplus jackets, zipped up over sweatshirts to keep out the cold and wind. Allerton seemed insubstantial as a phantom; Lee could almost see through him, to the empty phantom bus outside.

From Ambato to Puyo, along the edge of a gorge a thousand feet deep. There were waterfalls and forests and streams running down over the roadway, as they descended into the lush green valley. Several times the bus stopped to remove large stones that had slid down onto the road.

Lee was talking on the bus to an old prospector named Morgan, who had been thirty years in the jungle. Lee asked him about Ayahuasca.

'Acts on them like opium,' Morgan said. 'All my Indians use it. Can't get any work out of them for three days when they get on Ayahuasca.'

'I think there may be a market for it,' Lee said.

Morgan said, 'I can get any amount.'

They passed the prefabricated bungalows of Shell Mara. The Shell Company had spent two years and twenty million dollars, found no oil, and pulled out.

They got into Puyo late at night, and found a room in a ramshackle hotel near the general store. Lee and Allerton were too exhausted to speak, and they fell asleep at once.

Next day Old Man Morgan went around with Lee, trying to score for Ayahuasca. Allerton was still sleeping. They hit a wall of evasion. One man said he would bring some the following day. Lee knew he would not bring any.

They went to a little saloon run by a mulatto woman. She pretended not to know what Ayahuasca was. Lee asked if Ayahuasca was illegal. 'No,' said Morgan, 'but the people are suspicious of strangers.'

They sat there drinking aguardiente mixed with hot water and sugar and cinnamon. Lee said his racket was shrunk-down heads. Morgan figured they could start a head-shrinking plant. 'Heads rolling off the assembly line,' he said. 'You can't buy those heads at any price. The government forbids it, you know. The blighters were killing people to sell the heads.'

Morgan had an inexhaustible fund of old dirty jokes. He was talking about some local character from Canada.

'How did he get down here?' Lee asked.

Morgan chuckled. 'How did we all get down here? Spot of trouble in our own country, right?'

Lee nodded, without saying anything.

Old Man Morgan went back to Shell Mara on the afternoon bus to collect some money owed him. Lee talked to a Dutchman named Sawyer who was farming near Puyo. Sawyer told him there was an American botanist living in the jungle, a few hours out of Puyo.

'He is trying to develop some medicine. I forget the name. If he succeeds in concentrating this medicine, he says he will make a fortune. Now he is having a hard time. He has nothing to eat out there.'

Lee said, 'I am interested in medicinal plants. I may pay him a visit.'

'He will be glad to see you. But take along some flour or tea or something. They have nothing out there.'

Later Lee said to Allerton, 'A botanist! What a break. He is our man. We will go tomorrow.'

'We can hardly pretend we just happened by,' said Allerton. 'How are you going to explain your visit?'

'I will think of something. Best tell him right out I want to score for Yage. I figure maybe there is a buck in it for both for us. According to what I hear, he is flat on his ass. We are lucky to hit him in that condition. If he was in the chips and drinking champagne out of galoshes in the whorehouses of Puyo, he would hardly be interested to sell me a few hundred Sucres' worth of Yage. And, Gene, for the love of Christ, when we do overhaul this character, please don't say, "Doctor Cotter, I presume."'

The hotel room in Puyo was damp and cold. The houses across the street were blurred by the pouring rain, like a city under water. Lee was picking up articles off the bed and shoving them into a rubberized sack. A .32 automatic pistol, some cartridges wrapped in oiled silk, a small frying pan, tea and flour packed in cans and sealed with adhesive tape, two quarts of Puro.

Allerton said, 'This booze is the heaviest item, and the bottle's got like sharp edges. Why don't we leave it here?'

'We'll have to loosen his tongue,' Lee said. He picked up the sack and handed Allerton a shiny new machete.

'Let's wait till the rain stops,' said Allerton.

'Wait till the rain stops!' Lee collapsed on the bed with loud, simulated laughter. 'Haw haw haw! Wait till the rain stops! They got a saying down here, like "I'll pay you what I owe you when it stops raining in Puyo." Haw haw.'

'We had two clear days when we first got here.'

'I know. A latter-day miracle. There's a movement

on foot to canonize the local padre. *Vámonos, cabrón.*'

Lee slapped Allerton's shoulder and they walked out in the rain, slipping on the wet cobblestones of the main street.

The trail was corduroy. The wood of the trail was covered with a film of mud. They cut long canes to keep from slipping, but it was slow walking. High jungle with hardwood forest on both sides of the trail, and very little undergrowth. Everywhere was water, springs and streams and rivers of clear, cold water.

'Good trout water,' Lee said.

They stopped at several houses to ask where Cotter's place was. Everyone said they were headed right. How far? Two, three hours. Maybe more. Word seemed to have gone ahead. One man they met on the trail shifted his machete to shake hands and said at once, 'You are looking for Cotter? He is in his house now.'

'How far?' Lee asked.

The man looked at Lee and Allerton. 'It will take you about three hours more.'

They walked on and on. It was late afternoon now. They flipped a coin to see who would ask at the next house. Allerton lost.

'He says three more hours,' Allerton said.

'We been hearing that for the past six hours.'

Allerton wanted to rest. Lee said, 'No. If you rest, your legs get stiff. It's the worst thing you can do.'

'Who told you that?'

'Old Man Morgan.'

'Well, Morgan or no, I am going to rest.'

'Don't make it too long. It will be a hell of a note if we get caught short, stumbling over snakes and jaguars in the dark and falling into *quebrajas* – that's what they call these deep crevices cut by streams of water. Some of them are sixty feet deep and four feet wide. Just room enough to fall in.'

They stopped to rest in a deserted house. The walls were gone, but there was a roof that looked pretty sound. 'We could stop here in a pinch,' said Allerton, looking around.

'A definite pinch. No blankets.'

It was dark when they reached Cotter's place, a small thatched hut in a clearing, Cotter was a wiry little man in his middle fifties. Lee observed that the reception was a bit cool. Lee brought out the liquor, and they all had a drink. Cotter's wife, a large, strong-looking, red-haired woman, made some tea with cinnamon to cut the kerosene taste of the Puro. Lee got drunk on three drinks.

Cotter was asking Lee a lot of questions. 'How did you happen to come here? Where are you from? How long have you been in Ecuador? Who told you about me? Are you a tourist or travelling on business?'

Lee was drunk. He began talking in junky lingo, explaining that he was looking for Yage, or Aya-huasca. He understood the Russians and the Americans were experimenting with this drug. Lee said he figured there might be a buck in the deal for both of them. The more Lee talked, the cooler Cotter's manner became. The man was clearly suspicious, but why or of what, Lee could not decide.

Dinner was pretty good, considering the chief ingredient was a sort of fibrous root and bananas. After dinner, Cotter's wife said, 'These boys must be tired, Jim.'

Cotter led the way with a flashlight that developed power by pressing a lever. A cot about thirty inches wide made of bamboo slats. 'I guess you can both make out here,' he said. Mrs. Cotter was spreading a blanket on the cot as a mattress, with another blanket as cover. Lee lay down on the cot next to the wall. Allerton lay on the outside, and Cotter adjusted a mosquito net.

'Mosquitos?' Lee asked.

'No, vampire bats,' Cotter said shortly. 'Good night.'

'Good night.'

Lee's muscles ached from the long walk. He was very tired. He put one arm across Allerton's chest, and snuggled close to the boy's body. A feeling of deep tenderness flowed out from Lee's body at the warm contact. He snuggled closer and stroked Allerton's shoulder gently. Allerton moved irritably, pushing Lee's arm away.

'Slack off, will you, and go to sleep,' said Allerton. He turned on his side, with his back to Lee. Lee drew his arm back. His whole body contracted with the shock. Slowly he put his hand under his cheek. He felt a deep hurt, as though he were bleeding inside. Tears ran down his face.

He was standing in front of the Ship Ahoy. The place looked deserted. He could hear someone crying. He saw his little son, and knelt down and took the child in his arms. The sound of crying came closer, a wave of sadness, and now he was crying, his body shaking with sobs.

He held little Willy close against his chest. A group of people were standing there in convict suits. Lee wondered what they were doing there and why he was crying.

When Lee woke up, he still felt the deep sadness of his dream. He stretched out a hand towards Allerton, then pulled it back. He turned around to face the wall.

Next morning, Lee felt dry and irritable and empty of feeling. He borrowed Cotter's .22 rifle and set out with Allerton to have a look at the jungle. The jungle seemed empty of life.

'Cotter says the Indians have cleaned most of the game out of the area,' said Allerton. 'They all have shotguns from the money they made working for Shell.'

They walked along a trail. Huge trees, some over a hundred feet high, matted with vines, cut off the sunlight.

'May God grant we kill some living creature,' Lee said. 'Gene, I hear something squawking over there. I'm going to try and shoot it.'

'What is it?'

'How should I know? It's alive, isn't it?'

Lee pushed through the undergrowth beside the trail. He tripped on a vine and fell into a saw-toothed plant. When he tried to get up, a hundred sharp points caught his clothes and stuck into his flesh.

'Gene!' he called. 'Help me! I been seized by a

man-eating plant. Gene, cut me free with the machete!'

They did not see a living animal in the jungle.

Cotter was supposedly trying to find a way to extract curare from the arrow poison the Indians used. He told Lee there were yellow crows to be found in the region, and yellow catfish with extremely poisonous spines. His wife had gotten spined, and Cotter had to administer morphine for the intense pain. He was a medical doctor.

Lee was struck by the story of the Monkey Woman: a brother and sister had come down to this part of Ecuador, to live the simple healthful life on roots and berries and nuts and palm hearts. Two years later a search-party had found them, hobbling along on improvised crutches, toothless and suffering from half-healed fractures. It seems there was no calcium in the area. Chickens couldn't lay eggs, there was nothing to form the shell. Cows gave milk, but it was watery and translucent, with no calcium in it.

The brother went back to civilization and steaks, but the Monkey Woman was still there. She earned her monicker by watching what monkeys ate: anything a monkey eats, she can eat, anybody can eat. It's a handy thing to know. It's a handy thing to know, if you get lost in the jungle. Also handy to bring along some calcium tablets. Even Cotter's wife had lost her teeth 'inna thervith.' His were long gone.

He had a five-foot viper guarding his house from prowlers after his precious curare notes. He also had two tiny monkeys, cute but ill-tempered and equipped with sharp little teeth, and a two-toed sloth. Sloths live on fruit in trees, swinging along upside down and making a sound like a crying baby. On the ground they are helpless. This one just lay there and thrashed about and hissed. Cotter warned them not to touch it, even on the back of the neck, since it could reach around with its strong, sharp claws and drive them through one's hand, then pull it to its mouth and start biting.

Cotter was evasive when Lee asked about Ayahuasca. He said he was not sure Yage and Ayahuasca were the same plant. Ayahuasca was connected with *Brujería* – witchcraft. He himself was a white *Brujo*. He had access to *Brujo* secrets. Lee had no such access.

'It would take you years to gain their confidence.'

Lee said he did not have years to spend on the deal. 'Can't you get me some?' he asked.

Cotter looked at him sourly. 'I have been out here three years,' he said.

Lee tried to come on like a scientist. 'I want to investigate the properties of the drug,' he said. 'I am willing to take some as an experiment.'

Cotter said, 'Well, I could take you down to Canela and talk to the *Brujo*. He will give you some if I say so.'

'That would be very kind,' said Lee.

Cotter did not say any more about going to Canela. He did say a lot about how short they were on supplies, and how he had no time to spare from his experiments with a curare substitute. After three days Lee saw he was wasting time, and told Cotter they were leaving. Cotter made no attempt to conceal his relief.

Epilogue:
Mexico City Return

Every time I hit Panama, the place is exactly one month, two months, six months more nowhere, like the course of a degenerative illness. A shift from arithmetical to geometrical progression seems to have occurred. Something ugly and ignoble and sub-human is cooking in this mongrel town of pimps and whores and recessive genes, this degraded leech on the Canal.

A smog of bum kicks hangs over Panama in the wet heat. Everyone here is telepathic on the paranoid level. I walked around with my camera and saw a wood and corrugated iron shack on a limestone cliff in Old Panama, like a penthouse. I wanted a picture of this excrescence, with the albatrosses and vultures wheeling over it against the hot gray sky. My hands holding the camera were slippery with sweat, and my shirt stuck to my body like a wet condom.

An old hag in the shack saw me taking the picture. They always know when you are taking their picture, especially in Panama. She went into an angry consultation with some other ratty-looking people I could not see clearly. Then she walked to the edge of a perilous balcony and made an ambiguous gesture of hostility.

Many so-called primitives are afraid of cameras. There is in fact something obscene and sinister about photography, a desire to imprison, to incorporate, a sexual intensity of pursuit. I walked on and shot some boys – young, alive, unconscious – playing baseball. They never glanced in my direction.

Down by the waterfront I saw a dark young Indian on a fishing boat. He knew I wanted to take his picture, and every time I swung the camera into position he would look up with young male sulkiness. I finally caught him leaning against the bow of the boat with languid animal grace, idly scratching one shoulder. A long white scar across right shoulder and collarbone. I put away my camera and leaned over the hot concrete wall, looking at him. In my mind I was running a finger along the scar, down across his naked copper chest and stomach, every cell aching with deprivation. I pushed away from the wall muttering 'Oh Jesus' and walked away, looking around for something to photograph.

A Negro with a felt hat was leaning on the porch rail of a wooden house built on a dirty limestone foundation. I was across the street under a movie marque. Every time I prepared my camera he would lift his hat and look at me, muttering insane imprecations. I finally snapped him from behind a pillar. On a balcony over this character a shirtless young man was washing. I could see the Negro and Near Eastern blood in him, the rounded face and *café-au-lait* mulatto skin, the smooth body of undifferentiated flesh with not a muscle showing. He looked up from his washing like an animal scenting danger. I caught him when the five o'clock whistle blew. An old photographer's trick: wait for a distraction.

I went into Chico's Bar for a rum Coke. I never liked this place, nor any other bar in Panama, but it used to be endurable and had some good numbers on the juke box. Now there was nothing but this awful Oklahoma honky-tonk music, like the bellowings of an anxious cow: 'You're Drivin' Nails in my Coffin' – 'It Wasn't God Made Honky Tonk Angels' – 'Your Cheatin' Heart.'

The servicemen in the joint all had that light-concussion Canal Zone look: cow-like and blunted, as if they had undergone special G.I. processing and were immunized against contact on the intuition level, telepathic sender and receiver excised. You ask them a question, they answer without friendliness or hostility. No warmth, no contact. Conversation is impossible. They just have nothing to say. They sit around buying drinks for the B-girls, making lifeless passes which the girls brush off like flies, and playing that whining music on the juke box. One young man with a pimply adenoidal face kept trying to touch a girl's breast. She would brush his hand away, then it would creep back as if endowed with autonomous insect life.

A B-girl sat next to me, and I bought her one drink. She ordered good Scotch, yet. 'Panama, how I hate your cheatin' guts,' I thought. She had a shallow bird brain and perfect Stateside English, like a recording. Stupid people can learn a language quick and easy because there is nothing going on in there to keep it out.

She wanted another drink. I said 'No.'

She said, 'Why are you so mean?'

I said, 'Look, if I run out of money, who is going to buy my drinks? Will you?'

She looked surprised, and said slowly, 'Yes. You are right. Excuse me.'

I walked down the main drag. A pimp seized my

arm. 'I gotta fourteen-year-old girl, Jack. Puerto Rican. How's about it?'

'She's middle-aged already,' I told him. 'I want a six-year-old virgin and none of that sealed-while-you-wait shit. Don't try palming your old fourteen-year-old bats off on me.' I left him there with his mouth open.

I went into a store to price some Panama hats. The young man behind the counter started singing: 'Making friends, losing money.'

'This spic bastard is strictly on the chisel,' I decided.

He showed me some two-dollar hats. 'Fifteen dollars,' he said.

'Your prices are way out of line,' I told him, and turned and walked out. He followed me into the street: 'Just a minute, Mister.' I walked on.

That night I had a recurrent dream: I was back in Mexico City, talking to Art Gonzalez, a former roommate of Allerton's. I asked him where Allerton was, and he said, 'In Agua Diente.' This was somewhere south of Mexico City, and I was inquiring about a bus connection. I have dreamed many times I was back in Mexico City, talking to Art or Allerton's best friend, Johnny White, and asking where he was.

I flew up to Mexico City. I was a little nervous going through the airport; some cop or Immigration inspector might spot me. I decided to stick close to the attractive young tourist I had met on the plane. I had packed my hat, and when I got off the plane I took off my glasses. I slung my camera over my shoulder.

'Let's take a cab into town. Split the fare. Cheaper that way,' I said to my tourist. We walked through the airport like father and son. 'Yes,' I was saying, 'that old boy in Guatemala wanted to charge me two dollars from the Palace Hotel out to the airport. I told him *uno.*' I held up one finger. No one looked at us. Two tourists.

We got into a taxi. The driver said twelve pesos for both to the center of town.

'Wait a minute,' the tourist said in English. 'No meter. Where your meter? You got to have a meter.'

The driver asked me to explain that he was authorized to carry airline passengers to town without a meter.

'No!' the tourist shouted. 'I not tourist. I live in Mexico City. *¿Sabe* Hotel Colmena? I live in Hotel Colmena. Take me to town but I pay what is on meter. I call police. *Policía.* You're required by law to have a meter.'

'Oh God,' I thought. 'That's all I need, this jerk should call the law.' I could see cops accumulating around the cab, not knowing what to do and calling other cops. The tourist got out of the cab with his suitcase. He was taking down the number.

'I call *policía* plenty quick,' he said.

I said, 'Well, I think I'll take this cab anyway. Won't get into town much cheaper . . . *Vámonos,*' I said to the driver.

I checked into an eight-peso hotel near Sears, and walked over to Lola's, my stomach cold with excitement. The bar was in a different place, redecorated, with new furniture. But there was the same old bartender behind the bar, with his gold tooth and his moustache.

'*¿Cómo está?*' he said. We shook hands. He asked where I had been, and I told him South America. I sat down with a Delaware Punch. The place was empty, but someone I knew was bound to come in sooner or later.

The Major walked in. A retired Army man,

gray-haired, vigorous, stocky. I ran through the list crisply with the Major:

'Johnny White, Russ Morton, Pete Crowly, Ike Scranton?'

'Los Angeles, Alaska, Idaho, don't know, still around. He's always around.'

'And oh, uh, whatever happened to Allerton?'

'Allerton? Don't believe I know him.'

'See you.'

''Night, Lee. Take it easy.'

I walked over to Sears and looked through the magazines. In one called *Balls: For Real Men*, I was looking at a photo of a Negro hanging from a tree: 'I Saw Them Swing Sonny Goons.' A hand fell on my shoulder. I turned, and there was Gale, another retired Army man. He had the subdued air of the reformed drunk. I ran through the list.

'Most everybody is gone,' Gale said. 'I never see those guys anyway, never hang around Lola's anymore.'

I asked about Allerton.

'Allerton?'

'Tall skinny kid. Friend of Johnny White and Art Gonzalez.'

'He's gone too.'

'How long ago?' No need to play it cool and casual with Gale. He wouldn't notice anything.

'I saw him about a month ago on the other side of the street.'

'See you.'

'See you.'

I put the magazine away slowly and walked outside and leaned against a post. Then I walked back to Lola's. Burns was sitting at a table, drinking a beer with his maimed hand.

'Hardly anybody around. Johnny White and Tex and Crosswheel are in Los Angeles.'

I was looking at his hand.

'Did you hear about Allerton?' he asked.

I said, 'No.'

'He went down to South America or some place. With an Army colonel. Allerton went along as guide.'

'So? How long has he been gone?'

'About six months.'

'Must have been right after I left.'

'Yeah. Just about then.'

I got Art Gonzalez's address from Burns and went over to see him. He was drinking a beer in a shop across from his hotel, and called me over. Yes, Allerton left about five months ago and went along as guide to a colonel and his wife.

'They were going to sell the car in Guatemala. A '48 Cadillac. I felt there was something not quite right about the deal. But Allerton never told me anything definite. You know how he is.' Art seemed surprised I had not heard from Allerton. 'Nobody has heard anything from him since he left. It worries me.'

I wondered what he could be doing, and where. Guatemala is expensive, San Salvador expensive and jerkwater. Costa Rica? I regretted not having stopped off in San José on the way up.

Gonzalez and I went through the where-is-so-and-so routine. Mexico City is a terminal of space-time travel, a waiting room where you grab a quick drink while you wait for your train. That is why I can stand to be in Mexico City or New York. You are not stuck there; by the fact of being there at all, you are travelling. But in Panama, crossroads of the world, you are exactly so much aging tissue. You have to make arrangements with Pan Am or the Dutch Line for removal of your body. Otherwise, it would stay there and rot in the muggy heat, under a galvanized iron roof.

That night I dreamed I finally found Allerton, hiding out in some Central American backwater. He seemed surprised to see me after all this time. In the dream I was a finder of missing persons.

'Mr. Allerton, I represent the Friendly Finance Company. Haven't you forgotten something, Gene? You're supposed to come and see us every third Tuesday. We've been lonely for you in the office. We don't like to say "Pay up or else." It's not a friendly thing to say. I wonder if you have ever read the contract *all the way through*? I have particular reference to Clause 6(x) which can only be deciphered with an electron microscope and a virus filter. I wonder if you know just what "**or else**" means, Gene?

'Aw, I know how it is with you young kids. You get chasing after some floozie and forget all about Friendly Finance, don't you? But Friendly Finance doesn't forget you. Like the song say, "No hiding place down there." Not when the old Skip Tracer goes out on a job.'

The Skip Tracer's face went blank and dreamy. His mouth fell open, showing teeth hard and yellow as old ivory. Slowly his body slid down in the leather armchair until the back of the chair pushed his hat down over his eyes, which gleamed in the hat's shade, catching points of light like an opal. He began humming 'Johnny's So Long at the Fair' over and over. The humming stopped abruptly, in the middle of a phrase.

The Skip Tracer was talking in a voice languid and intermittent, like music down a windy street. 'You meet all kinds on this job, Kid. Every now and then some popcorn citizen walks in the office and tries to pay Friendly Finance with *this* shit.'

He let one arm swing out, palm up, over the side of the chair. Slowly he opened a thin brown hand, with purple-blue fingertips, to reveal a roll of yellow thousand-dollar bills. The hand turned over, palm down, and fell back against the chair. His eyes closed.

Suddenly his head dropped to one side and his tongue fell out. The bills dropped from his hand, one after the other, and lay there crumpled on the red tile floor. A gust of warm spring wind blew dirty pink curtains into the room. The bills rustled across the room and settled at Allerton's feet.

Imperceptibly the Skip Tracer straightened up, and a slit of light went on behind the eyelids.

'Keep that in case you're caught short, Kid,' he said. 'You know how it is in these spic hotels. You gotta carry your own paper.'

The Skip Tracer leaned forward, his elbows on his knees. Suddenly he was standing up, as if tilted out of the chair, and in the same upward movement he pushed the hat back from his eyes with one finger. He walked to the door and turned, with his right hand on the knob. He polished the nails of his left hand on the lapel of his worn glen plaid suit. The suit gave out an odor of mold when he moved. There was mildew under the lapels and in the trouser cuffs. He looked at his nails.

'Oh, uh ... about your, uh ... account. I'll be around soon. That is, within the next few ...' The Skip Tracer's voice was muffled.

'We'll come to *some* kind of agreement.' Now the

voice was loud and clear. The door opened and wind blew through the room. The door closed and the curtains settled back, one curtain trailing over a sofa as though someone had taken it and tossed it there.

William Burroughs
Cities of the Red Night £3.95

His most important book since *The Naked Lunch*

'An obsessive landscape which lingers in the mind as a fundamental statement about the possibilities of human life'
PETER ACKROYD, SUNDAY TIMES

'Not only Burroughs' best work, but a logical and ripening extension of all Burroughs' great work' KEN KESEY

'Burroughs is an awe-inspiring poetic magician. I believe *Cities of the Red Night* is his masterpiece' CHRISTOPHER ISHERWOOD

'The outrageousness of *Cities of the Red Night* suggests it was written in collusion with Swift, Baudelaire, Schopenhauer, Orwell, Lenny Bruce, General Patton and John Calvin' SAN FRANCISCO HERALD

edited and introduced by John Calder
A William Burroughs Reader £3.95

It is a measure of Burroughs' influence and importance as a writer that the very titles of his books have found their way into contemporary language and consciousness: *The Naked Lunch, The Soft Machine, The Ticket That Exploded, Love Express, The Wild Boys, Exterminator!* This Reader contains substantial extracts from all Burroughs' work, edited and arranged to provide the perfect introduction to this most ferocious and apocalyptic of visionaries.

'A master of dialogue, a creator of character without contemporary equal, a humorist who gets funnier as his subject-matter gets blacker, and a first-class storyteller' JOHN CALDER

'The most radical innovator in fiction since Joyce, and probably of comparable importance' ANGELA CARTER, GUARDIAN

edited by John Calder
A Henry Miller Reader £3.95

In the words of Malcolm Bradbury, Henry Miller 'aimed to reverse or affront all tendencies and values of the decade . . . He is rightly seen now as a forerunner of post-war experimentation and post-modernism.'

This new compilation of Miller's work covers a large range of his writing from his youth to his later years.

'Henry Miller's work is one long autobiographical wrestle with world, flesh, devil and angel' DAILY TELEGRAPH

'American literature begins and ends with the meaning of what Miller has done' LAWRENCE DURRELL

edited by John Calder
A Samuel Beckett Reader £3.95

'The more he shrinks his world the more he enlarges it. The more he hides himself, the more he reveals himself, and our own situation takes on a new aspect. The more he wallows in the muck the more he extends our idea of beauty' – John Calder in his Introduction.

'There is no writer of our language with a tenth of Beckett's apprehension of what language can do. The experience of reading him is an extraordinary intersection of time and the timeless . . . an art of contemplation is revived' CHRISTOPHER RICKS

'He is the most courageous, remorseless writer going . . . the finest writer writing' HAROLD PINTER

'Last of the giants . . . the last of the modernists . . . above and beyond literary fashion' THE TIMES

All these books are available at your local bookshop or newsagent, or can be ordered direct from the publisher. Indicate the number of copies required and fill in the form below.

Send to: **CS Department, Pan Books Ltd., P.O. Box 40,
            Basingstoke, Hants.   RG21 2YT.**

or phone: 0256 469551 (Ansaphone), quoting title, author
            and Credit Card number.

Please enclose a remittance* to the value of the cover price plus: 60p for the first book plus 30p per copy for each additional book ordered to a maximum charge of £2.40 to cover postage and packing.

*Payment may be made in sterling by UK personal cheque, postal order, sterling draft or international money order, made payable to Pan Books Ltd.

Alternatively by Barclaycard/Access:

Card No.

Signature:

Applicable only in the UK and Republic of Ireland.

While every effort is made to keep prices low, it is sometimes necessary to increase prices at short notice. Pan Books reserve the right to show on covers and charge new retail prices which may differ from those advertised in the text or elsewhere.

NAME AND ADDRESS IN BLOCK LETTERS PLEASE:

....

Name

Address

3/87